Crab Campaign

An Invasive Species Tracker's Journal

Book design by Jake Slavik
Illustrations by Arpad Olbey (Beehive Illustration)

Design Elements: Shutterstock Images

Published in the United States by Jolly Fish Press, an imprint of North Star Editions, Inc.

First Edition
First Printing, 2019

This is a work of fiction. Names, characters, places, and incidents are either the product of the author's imagination or are used fictitiously, and any resemblance to actual persons living or dead, business establishments, events, or locales is entirely coincidental.

Library of Congress Cataloging-in-Publication Data
Names: Watson, J. A., 1980- author. | Olbey, Arpad, illustrator.
Title: Crab campaign : an invasive species tracker's journal / by J. A. Watson ; illustrations by Arpad Olbey.
Description: First edition. | Mendota Heights, MN : Jolly Fish Press, an imprint of North Star Editions, Inc., 2020. | Series: Science Squad | Summary: "Ned convinces the Science Squad to spend their summer tracking down an invasive species that might be threatening the Chesapeake Bay, the elusive Chinese Mitten Crab"— Provided by publisher.
Identifiers: LCCN 2018050126 (print) | LCCN 2018053908 (ebook) | ISBN 9781631632976 (e-book) | ISBN 9781631632969 (pbk.) | ISBN 9781631632952 (hardcover)
Subjects: | CYAC: Chinese mitten crab—Fiction. | Crabs—Fiction. | Biological invasions—Fiction. | Science projects—Fiction. | Chesapeake Bay (Md. and Va.)—Fiction. | LCGFT: Fiction.
Classification: LCC PZ7.1.W4155 (ebook) | LCC PZ7.1.W4155 Cr 2019 (print) | DDC [Fic]—dc23
LC record available at https://lccn.loc.gov/2018050126

Jolly Fish Press
North Star Editions, Inc.
2297 Waters Drive
Mendota Heights, MN 55120
www.jollyfishpress.com

Printed in the United States of America

Crab Campaign

An Invasive Species Tracker's Journal

by J. A. Watson

Illustrations by Arpad Olbey (Beehive Illustration)

Text by Mary C. Wild

Consultant: Dr. Andrew A. David,
Assistant Professor of Biology, Clarkson University

JOLLY
FiSH
PRESS

Mendota Heights, Minnesota

Prediction:
Boring Summer

This summer is going to be so boring, I'm sure of it. I probably won't even bother to write in this journal much since I'm going to be stuck here in Maryland when I could be packing my bags for China. And to think I had such high hopes. How naïve I was . . .

It all started yesterday when Mom, Dad, and I were eating at House of Noodles to celebrate the end of the school year and the A+ for my report on the Terra-Cotta Warriors. (Side note: I may be a B student, but it would have been pretty pathetic if I didn't get an A+ on my report. I mean, a whole army of life-size clay soldiers buried with an emperor?! That's wicked cool!). Anyway, back to why this summer is going to be so awful. You know how fortune cookies say dumb things like "Your only way to have a friend is to be one"? Things that aren't even predictions, more like observations? The one I got at House of Noodles yesterday was definitely true and an actual prediction. It had to be! It said, "You will step on the soil of many countries." All semester I've been wanting to go to China and see those Terra-Cotta Warriors. And now, to get that fortune while out celebrating my hard work—it had to be a sign! Right?

Wrong. When I told my parents why I was so excited about my fortune, they were amazed, and not in a good way. They didn't buy into the idea at all that a little piece of paper was a sure sign I was going to China, at least not anytime soon. What did they need it to say: "Hello, Ned Bolling, you will step on the soil of many countries"?

Instead, they had all kinds of practical questions, like how would I pay for it and what about my responsibilities at home and with the Science Squad. Okay, so it's true that I'm the new leader of the Eastern Shore Science Squad. Maggie was supposed to be, but her family had to move to Boston for her dad's job. My plans to travel the world *and* be the leader of the Eastern Shore Science Squad cancel each other out.

If I'm not going to China this summer, all I want to do is swing in the hammock on our porch and read the books that I lugged home from the library on the

Terra-Cotta Warriors. The thing I'm most interested in is their weapons. They had the coolest arrowheads . . .

Here's the crazy part: Those arrowheads, which archaeologists think are from the third century BCE, look a lot like the ones I collect around here, which are even older! Paleo-Indians were the first Marylanders. Archaeologists say they migrated to North America more than 10,000 years ago to hunt mammoth, bison, and caribou. I never really thought about *where* they were migrating from, so I looked it up. Get this: These people, who were of Asian descent, crossed the land bridge into the Alaska-Canada area of North America!

Okay, so maybe they weren't from China exactly, but still I like to discover connections between things that, when you first look at them, don't seem connected at all, like arrowheads from two different continents. My parents call this "daydreaming." Dad says it's what keeps me from being "productive," which translates to he thinks I don't help out enough on our farm. Dad inherited our farm from his dad, who inherited it from his dad. It's a small farm, but it's still a lot of work, which my dad points out to me just about every day. Even though he hires workers to help plant and harvest the crops, he

7

still expects me to help out, especially in the summer when school's out. I don't mind so much—when I have the time—but I have other stuff on my mind besides corn, peas, squash, and tomatoes. When I ask Mom why she doesn't help, she says she does "the books" and that she'd much rather take care of people than vegetables. Guess that's why she's a nurse.

I need to get my parents to see the big picture— the someday picture. Instead, they want to cramp my style with lists of chores I need to check off. At the very least, they should understand that I need to relax a little this summer. Mom has her book club, and Dad carves decoys of Eastern Shore ducks, paints them in colors that are true to life, and sells them in the stores in town. He says it "supplements his income." Mom says it gives him an excuse to hang out with his buddies at the woodworking shop.

Still, as the leader of the Guardians of the Bay (the name our Science Squad gave to ourselves), I probably should spend less time in the hammock and more time planning our next project. At least that should get Dad off my back . . .

Boring summer, here I come.

Invasion of the Mitten Crab

Maybe I was wrong about this summer. Maybe it'll be interesting after all.

Today, as I was drinking some of my mom's icy mint tea and hanging out in the hammock (no need to rush into this Squad leader business too quickly), Dad came racing around the corner of the house. He jumped onto the porch two steps at a time and waved a "Wanted: Dead or Alive" poster in front of my face. It had a picture of a fierce-looking crab on it. Its name: the Chinese mitten crab.

"I found this nailed to a pole down by the docks," he said. *"They're an invasive species that's wreaked havoc right here along the Chesapeake. Why don't you check out the website? Maybe you and the rest of the Guardians of the Bay should investigate these crabs this summer."*

In other words: Stop lying around and go do something!

<u>Chinese</u> mitten crabs? Talk about destiny!

I asked him to hand me the poster.

He said, "You can borrow it, but when you're done with it, return it."

I had to hold back an eye roll. "Put things back where you found them," he always says. Even though his advice gets old, he's often right.

After waiting a decent amount of time (I didn't want him to think I was too interested in his suggestion), I went to the Mitten Watch website listed on the poster.

Here's some of what I learned:

- The Chinese mitten crab is from East Asia and has hairy claws with white tips and a notch between its eyes. Its exoskeleton, called a carapace, is usually four inches wide in adults, and its legs are longer that its body is wide (just like me!). The scientific name, *Eriocheir sinensis*, translates as "wool hand, the Chinese." Their "mittens" are actually patches of bristles called setae (pronounced see-tee).

- This crab looks like a troublemaker, and it is! It eats other species' food and hogs their space, so it poses a special threat to the blue crab. It also causes erosion because it burrows into riverbanks, causing them to collapse.

- No one has reported seeing Chinese mitten crabs in the Chesapeake Bay since 2009, but that doesn't mean they aren't here!

There was other cool stuff on the website, too—fliers you can print out and mug shots of crabs that have been captured, where they were captured, and the date they were captured. My Squad could have a crab on that page someday!

There was also information on what to do if you find one, which is: "Do not throw it back into the water!" Looks like my dad's advice to put things back where you find them doesn't apply to Chinese mitten crabs. Ha!

Revised Prediction:
Awesome Summer

Breaking News: This summer is going to be <u>awesome</u>! I can't wait for Joey, Dante, and Elmer (he should be back in the States soon!) to hear about my idea for our Science Squad project. They're going to love it!

More to come later!

A Tough Crowd

I called the first meeting of the Science Squad today and shared all the interesting facts about Chinese mitten crabs that I've found so far.

In typical Joey fashion, she zeroed in on just one fact. "No one's seen these crabs since 2009?" she asked.

Joey and I have been friends since kindergarten. I can tell when her brain is clicking into high gear. She wants to be an investigative reporter someday so she can spend all her time digging for the truth.

"Right," I said.

"So, isn't it likely they just died?"

I explained what I'd learned so far—that invasive species don't usually just die out, especially when there are a lot of them. And that scientists believe it's more likely the Chinese mitten crabs are here, just under the radar.

Joey was less skeptical after I mentioned scientists, but she still wasn't convinced that hunting for these

crabs was the best choice for our project. She wants
to measure the bay's oxygen content and prevent a
crab jubilee. (When the water's oxygen content is too
low, blue crabs sometimes scuttle onto land to escape
suffocation. It's known as a "crab jubilee.") Joey's
parents are watermen, and they're worried they might
lose their jobs because of fewer blue crabs in the
Chesapeake Bay. So she wants to make sure we do
something again this year to protect the crabs. I want
that too. Just about everyone in our town depends on
the survival of the blue crab in some way.

Then there's Dante. He said he wants to pick
something dramatic this time, like documenting the
dangers of land development that's encroaching on our
bayside town, sending excess sediment into the water.
But isn't a fish-egg-eating crab that looks like it's
wearing mittens dramatic?!

As Guardians of the Bay, we ALL wanted to do
something again this year to protect the blue crab,
that was a no-brainer. The Squad and I earned badges
last summer for removing plastic containers and bags
from rivers and creeks that feed into the bay and for
preserving the underwater grasses.

Why can't Joey and Dante see the superiority of my idea?! I wish Elmer were here, but he's still in Mexico. He texted me last night that his dad is still waiting for his temporary visa to work at the seafood processing plant this summer. If the visa comes through, they both will travel to Maryland like they've done the last five summers.

For now, I'm going to suggest that Elmer can vote in absentia for our mitten crab tracker project. Joey and Dante had fine ideas but not as good as mine. Determining if an invasive species is still lurking in our bay should be the winner!

Mitten Crabs Beware

Dad says I have a way of buzzing around until I get my way. I don't know about that, but I definitely have been bitten by the travel bug. If I can't go China for a while, I can at least learn about a crab from there.

Yesterday's meeting didn't go very well, so Joey wants to "table our ideas" until next week. But I don't think we can wait that long. I convinced her and Dante to meet me at the marina at 10:00 a.m. sharp today.

When they both were finally assembled (at 10:03, I might add), I pointed to the poster.

"Guys," I said, "this crab definitely endangers our blue crabs. It tries to eat what blue crabs eat. And it burrows into riverbanks and causes erosion."

They must have talked on their meander over, because Dante immediately jumped on Joey's "but no one's seen one since 2009" bandwagon. Then he added that 2009 was practically before he was born. Dante needs to get better at math if he wants a job someday.

He says he wants to be a chef. I think that's because he loves to eat and he thinks he'll get free food.

Anyway, I was getting so frustrated with the lack of enthusiasm for what was obviously a great project, I said, "You both know scientists need hard evidence. It isn't likely that these nasty crabs have left our bay. They've probably gone undercover! It's imperative that we help solve the mystery of the Chinese mitten crabs gone missing."

It was at this point that Joey rolled her eyes. I couldn't quite hear what she muttered under her breath, but I think it was something like "There Ned goes, trying to be the boss of us again."

I chose to ignore her. I tried to remind them that our online profile pages on Science Squad HQ could get a lot of stickers. They still weren't convinced, but I persevered anyway.

Chinese mitten crabs have puzzled scientists on both the East and West Coasts. In 1992, fishers trawling for shrimp in San Francisco Bay were surprised to find a Chinese mitten crab in their catch. The crab's numbers in the bay quickly grew to the millions and remained high through 2005, but they haven't been seen in California since 2010. A Chesapeake Bay waterman reported finding a Chinese mitten crab in 2005, the first one spotted on the East Coast. There have been no reports of any in Maryland since 2009. The 2018 capture of one in New York has increased the likelihood that they'll show up again in the Chesapeake Bay or elsewhere.

I told them that when we find a Chinese mitten crab, we can't under any circumstances throw it back in the water. I figured that might get their attention.

"So, what are we supposed to do with it then?" Joey asked. "Keep it as a pet, like a hermit crab?"

I explained, as patiently as I could, that we'd need to freeze it until we could get it to a research center. Dante said his parents had a freezer in their basement that would be perfect. He was getting into it!

It was steamy on the dock, so I had to think fast. I told them we could use my dad's canoe, which is really cool because it's made of birch bark, to poke around in rivers and creeks. (I don't have permission to borrow it, but I'll figure that part out later.) And for good measure, I promised to persuade some very special guests to come to our scouting parties. (I have no idea who that will be, but I figure I'll think of something.)

Finally, Joey and Dante agreed. I texted Elmer, and he was in too. And as soon as I got home, I registered our project on Science Squad HQ before they could change their minds.

So it's official: We're going for an Invasive Species badge this summer!

Lining Up Support

Today's first order of business as mitten crab trackers was to line up a sponsor. We all agreed that Ms. Tinsley, Joey's and my fifth grade teacher and our mentor last year, would be perfect. Plus, she'll probably be Dante's teacher next year so it just makes sense.

We walked over to our school, hoping Ms. Tinsley would be there, packing up her classroom stuff. "Did you guys miss school so much you're ready to come back?" she asked.

Um, no. School's okay, but I'd much rather be spending summer break working on this great project.

Since I was the most psyched about our project, I did the majority of the talking. I told Ms. Tinsley how destructive the Chinese mitten crabs are.

"Fascinating!" she said. "I'd love to be your mentor again, but I'm not sure I have time for that this summer. I have my hands pretty full right now." She pointed to a gigantic pile of papers on her desk. "But I'd love it if you kids could educate me on your findings. I've never heard of Chinese mitten crabs before."

Leave it to Ms. T. to suggest we educate others on the topic. She did help us earn a lot of stickers last year, but it doesn't matter if we don't have a mentor on our project . . .

She must have noticed the disappointment on our faces because she added, "But I'm happy to help you find a mentor."

"Really?!" I said. "That'd be great!"

Located where land meets water, wetlands act like a sponge, soaking up pollutants and absorbing floodwaters. Hundreds of aquatic species—including worms, snails, mussels, tiny crustaceans, snakes, turtles, and frogs—thrive in tidal wetlands. Birds and mammals (both large and small) depend on wetlands for food and shelter. Shoreline development, a rising sea level, and invasive species pose major threats to the Chesapeake Bay wetlands.

She told us that she volunteers with scientists at the Eastern Shore Biological Research Lab, and she knows the perfect person there to mentor us. Yay, Ms. Tinsley (even if you only gave me a B in science)!

Ms. Tinsley pulled up the lab's website on her laptop and looked up Dr. Maureen Bryant, a marine biologist who specializes in invasive species. I signed on to my email account (being the leader of the Squad), and we worked together to compose an email asking Dr. Bryant to be our mentor. I included Ms. Tinsley's name in it, too, as a reference.

I got an answer back a few hours ago from Dr. Bryant.

"This is serendipitous*," she wrote. "We're on the lookout for the Chinese mitten crabs and so are several other organizations. But you're the first citizen scientists who've contacted me." She said to call her Dr. Mo. And get this: She's inviting us to come aboard her research vessel next Tuesday when she docks at our town's marina. She wants to hear more about our project.

---

*serendipitous—a happy chance. Besides arrowheads, I like to collect words.

Joey's so excited she's been hopping around like, well, like a kangaroo. Her parents named her Joey because when she was born she was tiny and had sort of pointy ears, like a baby kangaroo. Guess that was better than naming her Elf!

I can't wait for next Tuesday! I hope Dr. Mo will agree to be our mentor, and I hope we get good news from Elmer that he's coming back to Maryland for the summer. The Squad isn't the same without him.

As catadromous creatures, Chinese mitten crabs spawn in salty water from late winter through early summer. Each female lays from 250,000 to one million eggs per brood. The eggs that survive develop into larvae, some of which then survive as juveniles. The juvenile crabs make their way upstream to fresh water, where they stay for one to three years before heading back downstream as mature adults to begin the cycle again.

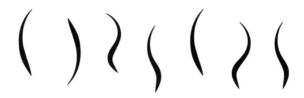

Dante's Idea Stinks

I have been finding buckets full of goopy, slimy stuff on our front porch. My parents are NOT amused. Neither am I. Those buckets stink!

Mom said something like it was bad enough that I fall behind on chores, now I was leaving lord knows what on the porch. They didn't want to hear that it was a mystery I was looking into. "Just get rid of it" was all Dad said.

So I called a Squad meeting. I wondered if Joey or Dante could help me get to the bottom of who was leaving that smelly stuff on our porch.

Turns out, solving the mystery was easier than I thought it would be. Dante confessed to being the mastermind behind the whole plot right away.

A few weeks back, he mentioned that he was working to recruit more people to join our Squad. Joey and I thought it was a great idea. We can always use more kids who love science and nature.

But it turns out that Dante had been telling his interested friends that finding a Chinese mitten crab was the initiation token you needed to get into our Squad. And he had designated the Bolling porch (but not his own, you notice) as a drop-off spot for "special science experiment materials."

He knows Science Squad doesn't have initiation fees. WHAT was he thinking?

"But I wasn't asking for money," Dante explained. "I was asking for a crab. I thought it would be a good way to have my own crew looking for them."

I asked why his "crew" didn't leave their junk at <u>his</u> house.

"We don't have a porch," he said. As if that was the only problem to his absurd scheme.

From all the seaweed, barnacles, shells, and little white crabs his Science Squad candidates left on our porch, it's obvious they don't know squat about mittens, because none of the buckets contained the furry-clawed crabs we're looking for. (We've decided to call Chinese mitten crabs just "mittens" since we're going to be talking about them so much.)

26

More Facts about Mittens

It seems like Tuesday will never get here! I can't wait to check out Dr. Mo's research vessel. In the meantime, I'm trying to learn all I can about the mittens.

Here's some more fascinating facts about them:

- They are catadromous, meaning they spend some of their time in brackish (a combination of salty and fresh) water like the bay and some of their time in fresh water.
- Unlike blue crabs, mittens aren't very good swimmers. (That's one thing I have in common with them—I can do the doggy paddle, but that's about it!)
- They sometimes walk on land to get around obstacles like dams or traps set up to capture them. Clever!
- They can walk eleven miles per hour, and they migrate up to 800 miles.
- They're sort of a brownish-green color.

We Have a Mentor!

Today was awesome! It was really hard to keep my cool when Dr. Mo's research vessel, *Baywatch*, pulled into the marina this morning. It was huge, and it had all kinds of contraptions on it. I stuffed my hands way into my pockets to look calm and collected. I had to. Joey was hopping up and down, and Dante was dancing around like mad.

Dr. Mo invited us on board, introduced us to her staff, and asked us to tell her more about our project. Finally, she said, "I would love to be your mentor." We were all so happy!

Then she showed us around. The first thing I noticed was something that almost looked a like a solar panel. Dr. Mo said it was a giant sieve for collecting specimens. She explained that they place things that don't fit through the sieve in a sample bottle and take it back to the lab for analysis.

"Now you must have some questions for me," she said. Boy, did we ever.

"Have you found any mittens?" Joey asked.

"Not yet," she said. "That's why we're asking for everyone's help. People are spending a lot of time on the water now that it's summer. If they know what to look for, they might spot one."

My main question was where we could find mittens. She told us that late winter through early summer is the best time to find the adults that are spawning in salt water, because they're large and easy to see.

"Then we should be out there looking for them right now," I said, to explain why I was starting to act all twitchy.

"Definitely," she said. "Keep your eyes open whenever you're near water. There could be a mitten lurking, especially if you're out crabbing."

She told us about another way we can really help with the search, which is by informing other citizens about it, and she asked us if we'd heard of crowdsourcing.

Joey knew what it was, but Dante and I weren't so sure. "So," Joey said in her know-it-all voice, "it's when a crowd of people—people who sometimes don't even know each other—all work together to solve a problem. Social media has a lot to do with it."

Dr. Mo says that she and her team are counting on crowdsourcing to make their mission a success. She figures if the mittens are out there and everyone is looking for them, there's a better chance of finding them.

Dante asked what to do when you capture one. I suspect he wasn't listening when I discussed all that earlier. So annoying.

She laid out the five steps:

1. Catch it (probably the trickiest part).

2. Take close-up photos of it.

3. Note where and when you found it.

4. Freeze it.

5. Get it to a lab as soon as possible.

He probably still wasn't listening today. I caught him eyeing a cooler stashed in a crowded corner of the boat. "Are they good to eat, like blue crabs?"

That's when Dr. Mo gave a little sigh. "We get asked that question a lot," she said. "People in China eat them, but it's complicated."

I made a note to investigate that, and Joey jotted something down too.

"For now," Dr. Mo continued, "we want people to record as much information as they can, then get the crabs to us."

Dr. Mo gave me her business card with her cell number and email address so we could keep in touch. When I asked if we could go with her, she said for now citizen scientists aren't allowed on Baywatch missions, but maybe someday.

She also gave us a pile of fliers to hand out to people and some "Wanted: Dead or Alive" posters like the one my dad found. She said to be sure to get permission before putting the fliers up in public places. The fliers have a picture of a mitten and "Have you seen me?" in big black letters. Underneath, there's info about what to do if you do see one and the URL for the Mitten Watch website.

Our first assignment as mitten trackers!

She gave us a box of bumper stickers too. They said, "Stop Aquatic Hitchhikers."

She told us she had those left over from a public awareness campaign about risks posed by zebra mussels.

I asked her if it had worked.

She said she thought it had, because there are fewer in the bay than there used to be. Seems more like *car*sourcing than *crowd*sourcing to me. Ha!

I sent a photo to Elmer of all of us standing by the super-sized sieve with Dr. Mo.

Before we left, she repeated the number one rule: "DONT THROW A MITTEN BACK INTO THE WATER."

Working the Crowd

I haven't written much because I've been so tired. We walked around town all week, putting up wanted posters and handing out fliers. There are always droves of tourists walking around, especially in summer, and most of them stopped to talk with us. Blue crabs and oysters used to be the major industries in our town. Now it's tourism. Crazy.

Most people had never even heard of the Chinese mitten crab, but they were pretty interested. The picture on the flier is dramatic. It definitely captures people's attention. So does Dooley, Dante's big, goofy Chesapeake Bay retriever, who Dante insisted would be a "conversation starter" if we brought him along. Sort of true. We put a "Maryland Is for Crabs" T-shirt on him. It seems like practically every tourist wears one of those. Dooley is super friendly, and kids especially want to pet him. But Dante has GOT to teach him to stop jumping on people. He almost knocked two people down!

We passed out some little orange stickers with "Find the Mittens!" on them to kids.

"Wish we could give out balloons too," Dante said. As soon as he said it, I knew Joey would be on his case.

"Balloons? Seriously? You know marine creatures will mistake deflated balloons for food or become tangled up in them. Either way, they'll die!"

I wish Dante would think before he speaks sometimes . . .

But that wasn't Joey's only agenda for the week. She must have thought our campaign to raise awareness was also a good time to do some investigating, because when we got to one of the most popular restaurants in town, she marched right in and asked to talk with the owner. I wanted to wait outside with Dante and Dooley, but Joey grabbed my arm to follow.

"Do you double-check the crab pieces you purchase to make sure there aren't any suspicious parts mixed in?" she asked. She had her notebook and pen out.

Just about every restaurant in town serves the famous blue crab in one dish or another, and I could see where she was going with this. I wished I was outside with Dante and Dooley.

The owner looked pretty annoyed. "That's the processing company's job, not mine," he said and hurried off.

What did Joey think? That a furry claw from a mitten would turn up floating in someone's crab soup or packed into someone's crab cake? From a logical standpoint, that doesn't seem likely.

When I told her that, Joey sighed and said, "An investigative reporter leaves no stone unturned." Then she pushed her glasses up on her nose.

Okay, so she had a point. At another restaurant, I slipped past the manager to talk with the workers in the kitchen. When I showed the flier, one of them said, "Yeah, I think I saw one of those crabs last year. Thought it had some disease or something. Its claws were so weird. I tossed it in the garbage."

Good grief! Never throw a suspicious crab away! We definitely need to keep handing out fliers!

So Many Questions

This past weekend we took a break from raising awareness. Dante had to take Dooley to obedience classes, Joey had music lessons, and I wanted to look for arrowheads. Not that I got much time to do that, because Dad wanted help hauling crops to the market yesterday.

But we were back at it on Monday. And it's a good thing. It seemed like no one had ever heard of mittens before! We heard the same questions over and over:

- "Can you eat them?" This is the question we were asked the most. We just said, "No." Then people would inevitably ask us why, and we had to admit we didn't know the reason.

- "Do they wear mittens to keep warm?" A lot of kids asked us this one. Seems like everyone likes the idea of crabs wearing mittens. We had to explain over and over that they don't actually wear mittens. It's just that their hairy claws kind of *look like mittens. As to why they have those hairy claws, I admitted more than once that we didn't really know the answer to that question. I tried the "What do YOU think?" trick that parents and teachers like to use. I just got blank stares.*

- *"Do they swim here from China?" We told them that they did not. We said that the mittens likely came as larvae in the tanks of ships, because that is what Dr. Mo had told us (she said something about "ballast water," which none of us were sure what that is). But we stopped there, because we didn't know too much more than that.*

- *"Why do we need to get rid of these crabs?" Out of all the questions we got, this one baffled me the most. I mean, shouldn't this be obvious?*

I deduced from our conversations that the public doesn't know all that much about invasive species: where they come from, how much damage they can do, or how hard it is to get rid of them. Dr. Mo told us that about 200 invasive species may live in the Chesapeake Bay Watershed. Hardly anyone knew that!

I suggested that we take a break and walk down to the docks and talk with some watermen. After all, they're the eyes and ears of the bay. Joey reminded me that fishers go out before sunrise and aren't back until early afternoon. She urged us to talk with her mom and dad (both watermen) and said she'll be happy to arrange a visit.

A lot of people crab in the bay just for fun or to catch a few blue crabs for dinner. We reminded boaters coming in to the docks that they should make sure they don't toss any mittens back into the water by mistake. We got a lot of eye rolls and shoulder shrugs. Clearly, people are not understanding the importance of doing their part.

On Thursday, we mixed things up a bit and biked over to the seafood processing plant on the edge of town. We were standing outside when the first shift ended. (Thanks to Elmer for that tip!) We handed out information, but most people didn't want to look at pictures of crabs after dissecting real ones all day. One lady did stop to talk with us though. She said she remembered the mittens' appearance in 2005 and that our project was "very worthwhile." She said she'd keep an eye out for furry claws. She told us she's been working at the plant for forty years. "When I was a child, we could work as crab pickers," she said. "That was before Maryland law required crab pickers to be at least sixteen."

"Why?" I asked.

"For one thing, we work with very sharp knives," she explained.

Cool! A job that lets you work with knives. If I still haven't come up with enough money to go to China by the time I'm sixteen, maybe I'll apply for a summer job here!

Rainy Day

The forecast said it was supposed to rain all day, so we decided to make it a library day. Once we were all assembled, I told Joey and Dante that I think the Squad needs to be better informed. How can we convince novices of the importance of the mitten hunt if we scientists don't have all the answers ourselves? I decided that we each needed to specialize in an area. We talked, and each of us have a topic to look into.

- Yours truly—mittens in China
- Joey—ballast water
- Dante—illegal trading

Then we talked about making catchy "Free Help" ads, announcing that we could sort through boaters' bushel baskets and look for mittens that may have slipped through unnoticed.

Joey and Dante got to work on the design of the ad and the wording, while I got to work on my research.

After a few hours, I suggested Joey and Dante stop working on the ads and focus on their assignments, which were due by COB (close of business) the next day. I thought saying COB made my request sound pretty professional. But they said I was being tyrannical. I eventually convinced them that being experts in our respective fields was more of a priority than working for free.

And secretly I am hoping for a leadership sticker.

Free Help

I almost forgot, here's what our "Free Help" ad looks like:

Dear Boaters:

The Chinese mitten crab, an invasive species that is threatening our beloved bay, can attach itself to your gear. Before you leave for the night, you should check carefully to make sure there are no Chinese mitten crabs mixed in with your blue crabs.

No time for that sort of chore after a long day on the water? We, the Eastern Shore Science Squad, Guardians of the Bay, are offering you **FREE HELP** regarding this important matter.

Here's what we can do for you:

- Come aboard and inspect your crabbing or fishing equipment (e.g., your nets, pots, traps, buckets, and baskets) for Chinese mitten crabs, which are smaller than blue crabs and you might not notice because you are too busy or tired.
- If we find one, we'll photograph it, freeze it, and get it to the proper authorities.

Thank you for doing your part to identify and wipe out this invasive species that threatens the food supply and habitat of our beloved blue crab. We'll be around the docks most afternoons. Look for the kids with the Chesapeake Bay retriever.

I think it looks pretty great. We plan to hand it out with our other "Wanted" posters. I want to get lots of copies printed on heavy blue paper. Blue is my go-to color, of course, because of the blue crabs. I'm not super happy with the overuse of the word "beloved," but I lost that argument. It can be lonely at the top.

Before we left, Dante said it would be no problem to get copies of our ad printed so we could hand them out to crabbers and other fishers coming back with their loot.

Enter Margaux
and Ballast Water

Today was a crazy day! It was overcast, and it
rained off and on, so it was perfect that we spent most
of it in the library.

Joey and I were there at ten o'clock, as planned,
when the doors opened. I wasn't too surprised that
Dante wasn't there; he'd texted earlier that morning to
say he'd be a little late. He didn't say why, but I figured
some complication with watching his sisters or Dooley.
While we were waiting, Joey busied herself setting up
her online presentation. I was beginning to feel a little
embarrassed. All I had were a few notes and some
pictures on my phone for my topic.

Twenty minutes went by before Dante waltzed in
with no apology for being late and with a girl we'd never
seen before.

"This is Margaux, spelled M-a-r-g-a-u-x," he said. "I met her when I rode my bike over to the new Edgewater Grande Resort. She wants to join our Squad."

Margaux nodded her head and made a small curtsy.

"Well, that's four of the six," Joey said under her breath.

I've known Joey long enough to know that she was referring to the six key questions of journalism. We knew who she was: Margaux. We knew when Dante met her and where he'd met her. He told us how he'd gotten to meet her, sort of. The big question was, what was Dante doing at the new resort? And why did he think this girl would make a good Science Squad member? I mean, he just met her.

Margaux told us she's very interested in protecting the environment, but that she doesn't know much about crabs. Fair enough. We voted her in as a Squad member. Even if she doesn't know much about crabs, we can always use more members. And Dante's stinky scheme hadn't yielded any committed candidates anyway.

I cleared my throat. "We need to get back to business," I said. I asked Joey to start.

Joey stood up, adjusted her glasses, and put up her first slide. "Invasive species often hitchhike to a new location by hanging out in ballast water."

"What is 'ballast water'?" Margaux asked.

Glad she did, because I was wondering the same thing.

Joey said she knew that we would ask that question. Then she put up her next slide to explain:

- Ballast water is water that large boats suck up to keep them stable. So, ships have tanks that can be filled with something heavy like water to improve stability and to keep them from flopping around.
- Ballast water can be teeming with all kinds of creatures. Many of them, like mitten larvae, can be harmful when they land in a new environment.

I thought that was pretty interesting. Joey seemed to really have a handle on this ballast business, but then her talk took a turn for the weird.

"So, this is how it works," she said. "Let's say you operate a big commercial shipping company heading out of Baltimore with cars that you're exporting to a country we'll call Jolandia."

Huh?

"The weight of those cars provides the ballast you need for a safe journey. When you get to Jolandia, you unload your cars, but all you're bringing back are beautifully made dresses with deep pockets in the front—just right to hold personal items in. Joey clothes, even pounds and pounds of them, don't weigh nearly as much as cars."

Joey clothes?

At this point, Dante and I were shooting each other bug-eyed looks, but Margaux looked enthralled.

I was trying to picture "Joey clothes" when Joey pointed at me and asked what would I do if my ship needed more ballast for the trip back to Baltimore. I said that I guessed I'd fill the tank with seawater.

"Correct! Very good!" she said to me. "And what could be floating around in that seawater?"

I saw where she was going with that question. "Invasive species like Chinese mitten crab larvae," I said.

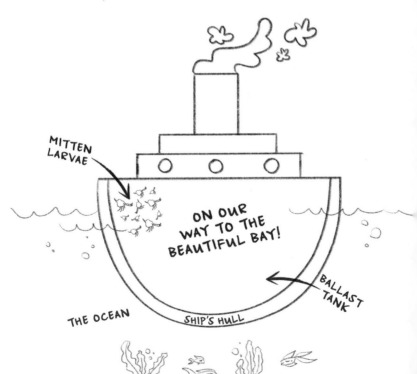

MITTEN LARVAE

ON OUR WAY TO THE BEAUTIFUL BAY!

BALLAST TANK

THE OCEAN

SHIP'S HULL

"Exactly. Now, what if a ship's ballast tank is loaded with all kinds of creepy crawlies on its way back to Baltimore? They can just keep on living there, right?"

"Right," Dante said a little too confidently.

"Wrong!" Joey shouted. "The ship has to dump that ballast water out when it gets to Baltimore because it will be loading fleets of cars into its hold and taking them back to Jolandia. It's a cycle that encourages the dispersal of invasive species as stowaways."

"That's really interesting," I said. "Is that true for cruise ships too?"

When Dante heard "cruise ships," he snapped to attention. He's been on one cruise his whole life, and that was with his parents over spring break, but I had a feeling he was going to pass himself off as an expert.

Sure enough, when Joey said that ships like the ones that come into the Port of Baltimore have ballast tanks to allow for changes in "fuel use and weight distribution," Dante had to add his two cents' worth.

"I totally get it about weight distribution," Dante said. "The way people on cruise ships always chow down at the dessert buffet, I'll bet they weigh way more coming back to port. You figure 3,000 people gaining seven pounds each, that's 20,000 more ballast pounds."

I couldn't resist shaking my head at that. *At least use a calculator, dude.*

Joey's on to Dante. "It's probably more complicated than that," she said, "but I found out that cruise ships have to meet discharge regulations just like every other type of ship. Any other questions?"

"I don't think so," I said, standing up. We needed to move on.

Margaux didn't pick up on my cue, however. She asked where she could buy a Jolandia dress because they sounded so cute (um, nowhere, Joey made them up) and if Dante's calculation for weight gain on a cruise includes souvenirs like clothes and jewelry, or just food consumed.

I can't write any more. My hand hurts, and besides, the conversation got just too off track.

Mittens in China and More Trouble

Okay, I just sat through dinner with my parents. My dad nagged the whole time about how he could use more help on the farm this summer. I tried to tell him how the Science Squad was taking up every free moment, but I'm not sure he bought it. And of course Mom was upset about her book club snacks (more on this later). Finishing up recording what happened in the library today seems much more enjoyable than enduring more awkward conversation with my parents. So here it goes . . .

My report "Mittens in China" was puny compared to Joey's. I wish I had gone first.

"Mittens are a delicacy in China," I began. "Restaurants serve them, and regular people buy them at the market live and take them home to steam for dinner."

"Besides outdoor markets," I continued, "you can buy the mittens in seafood stores. I saw a video of

51

one where there were whole tanks of them live and customers could pick out the ones they wanted. The merchant ties up the mittens' claws with heavy string so they're easier to cook."

I didn't have much information, but it was colorful, right?

"What kind of seasoning do they use?" Dante asked, always the chef.

I told him it was usually a sauce of ginger and vinegar, but I still hadn't shared the best part. "The most amazing thing is you can buy them in vending machines in places like subway stations. Sometimes, they're called Shanghai hairy crabs."

Joey didn't believe me, so I showed her the video on my phone. Instead of bags of potato chips or gummy worms, there were rows of crabs. Put in your money, and kerplunk! Down comes a little plastic see-through container holding a live mitten.

She wanted to know how much one would cost.

I told her I didn't know because I couldn't see how much *yuan* the man in the video puts into the machine. Guess I should have done a little more research.

Joey had another question. "Can you eat them right away, or do you have to take them home to steam them?"

I reminded her that they're alive but said that they are chilled so they won't move around much. And then I winged it, saying that maybe workers take them back to their offices and steam them in the microwave on their lunch breaks.

Joey pointed out the likelihood that putting a container like that in a microwave would probably result in crab guts spewed over its walls. It was at that point that Margaux covered her mouth with her hand and made a gagging sound.

Still, I soldiered on with a few more amazing facts to share. "Because the mittens are a delicacy in China, they are especially popular to enjoy at holidays like Chinese New Year," I explained. "People also give them to one another as gifts on ordinary occasions. I guess like people here give each other cookies."

Then I stopped to wait for applause.

"So that's it?" Dante asked.

I ignored him and instead asked Margaux if she had a topic she wanted to research. I suggested something easy, like maybe the mittens' burrows, just so she'd feel part of the Squad.

She gave me a deer-caught-in-the-headlights look but said she would try.

By that point we were getting angry knocks on the conference room door by the next group that had it signed out. So we all gathered our things to leave.

Once we were outside, I realized we had been cooped up in the windowless library conference room for nearly three hours—we had even missed lunch!

By that point I was STARVING, so I had this grand idea to invite everyone over to my house to celebrate Margaux as our new Squad member. Those "Free Help" ads could wait until tomorrow afternoon.

When we got to my house, I raided the pantry and found the perfect snack: fancy pretzels spiced with crab seasoning. And to drink, sparking apple cider.

Margaux was sneezing like crazy, I guess from the crab seasoning, which we put on everything around here. When she finally finished with her sneezing fit, she asked, "Why are you picking crabs for your topic? Crabs remind me of giant spiders."

I was happy to answer that question. I told her that we had picked the Chinese mitten crabs for this year's Science Squad project because they can hurt the blue crabs, and what hurts the blue crabs hurts all of us.

Margaux wanted to know why.

Joey gave the best answer: "If there are fewer blue crabs, then everyone who fishes for them and works on them and sells them and eats them is affected."

Before I realized it, we'd munched our way through two bags of pretzels. Pretzels make you thirsty, so we drank all the cider too.

After everyone left, I had the sinking feeling that those might have been treats my mom was saving for her book club meeting. Why hadn't I thought of that?

It didn't take long tonight for my mom to discover her "special" pretzels and drinks were missing. I guess the dead giveaway was that I left evidence in the family room where we'd been hanging out—glasses and empty bags and crumbs. Hence the other reason why dinner tonight was so awkward.

How Dante Met Margaux

Dante just called to tell me the story behind how he met Margaux. I think he felt like he owed me an explanation, being the leader of the Squad and all.

It sounds like he's still totally hung up on the perils of land development (his idea for this summer's badge), so he went to the newly opened Edgewater Grande Resort to snoop around and see if he could spot any suspicious-looking water being dumped into the bay or anything.

So this girl (Margaux) came up to him in the lobby and said her mom was the manager of the place and asked what he wanted. He told her that he was the vice president of Guardians of the Bay, explained what we do, and asked her if she'd be interested in joining.

"Vice president?" I repeated, incredulous. I mean really, Dante.

He got defensive and told me he couldn't help it— that he thought Margaux was cute.

I had no idea what to say to that. Dante didn't seem to sense my discomfort.

According to Dante, his VP title worked, because Margaux said she was very interested in joining the Squad. She called to her mom to ask about it. Dante explained this summer's project and how we were working to earn the Invasive Species badge.

Then he pointed to the library, which you could see from the back of the resort, and told her that the Squad was meeting right now.

Margaux's mom okayed the idea. Dante said she said something about how she wants Margaux to get community service credits this summer, to get a head start on them before school opens in September. But Dante confided in me that he thinks it's because of his winning argument.

I had nothing to say about that either.

Tomorrow's another library day with the Squad, so we agreed to meet at his house in the morning and walk over to the library together. I have to remember to bring my umbrella.

Laws and Burrows

When I got to Dante's house this morning, I had to do a double-take to make sure I was in the right place. He was dressed for his presentation like he was going to a wedding. He was wearing a blazer, nice pants, and nice shoes. This was weird for two reasons:

1. It's raining today (still).

2. He's strictly a T-shirt, shorts, and sneakers guy (like me).

I guess dressing up was what he meant yesterday when he said he'd be "more than ready" today. He's such a show-off!

When Dante and I made our entrance, Joey mouthed, "What the heck?" I just shrugged.

Dante got started on his report right away. We wanted to make sure we finished before we got kicked out again. He told us it was against the law to "import, export, sell, acquire, or purchase" invasive species under the Lacey Act. I couldn't imagine how you would just "acquire" a mitten. Like someone gave you one as a gift, maybe? Or you dipped your net into the bay one day and pulled one up?

"So, if federal agents catch you doing any of that illegal stuff, they'll throw you in jail?" Joey asked.

"I don't think so," Dante said. "But an individual who's caught with a mitten could be hit with a $100,000 misdemeanor fine. The fine can double if you're a company."

That's pretty serious.

When it was passed in 1900, the Lacey Act became the first federal law protecting wildlife. In 2008, the Lacey Act was amended. Today, it imposes strict penalties on anyone who imports plants and animals protected by international or domestic law and is intended to protect endangered species and prevent the spread of invasive ones. It is named for the congressman who first introduced it.

Joey asked about state laws.

Dante stood up tall and shot a quick glance at Margaux (probably trying to impress her) and read from his notes. Basically, the laws are the same as federal laws.

"You should see all the fishes and plants on the Maryland list besides the mitten," Dante said. "It could keep us in badges for years."

Margaux asked about the rules in other countries, like France.

Dante knew all about those too. He told us about a company that lost business selling tons of mittens to customers in Asia because it didn't follow the rules on invasive species.

I was floored with how much research Dante had done. He may have been trying to impress Margaux, but he definitely impressed me.

I quickly stood up to assume my leadership role.

"Fellow Science Squad members," I announced, "we need to be on the lookout, on our rivers and in our bay, for mitten thieves."

Dante and Joey gave my proposal a "Hear! Hear!" But Margaux didn't seem to be listening. She was hunched over our conference table, reading notes.

"Margaux," I said. "Your turn.

She looked up, bewildered. "Yes, okay." She shuffled some notes. "My talk is about burrows. Some cities have boroughs. For example, New York has five boroughs: Manhattan, Brooklyn, Queens, the Bronx, and Staten Island. I have lived in two of them, Manhattan and Brooklyn. They are both nice."

I was worried she had done her research on the wrong kind of "burrows," but then she said, "But I'm talking about burrows where animals and crabs live." Whew!

She told us the Latin name for the Chinese mitten crab is *Eriocheir sinensis*, which I already knew, and that mittens' burrows are oval-shaped and are found along sloping banks between the high tide mark and the low tide mark. She called the mittens "destructive crustaceans," then gave us the measurement of a burrow: one to three inches wide, up to eight inches deep, and one or two entrances. That didn't really mean much to me until she showed us a photograph of one.

"Sweet!" Dante and I said at the same time, then laughed. I was thinking it was a pretty good report for someone who had just joined the Squad, but it got even better.

She said the Chinese mitten crabs' burrows can "compromise the structural integrity of levees, and the crabs can even clog water distribution and power plant structures." Then she added that they've been a menace

on the Thames River in London, which her mother has
visited.

All this time we'd been telling people about the
damage mittens could do to blue crabs, not to humans.
Margaux's information about erosion was a way we
could get people riled up—make them see how it wasn't
just the crabs and other bay creatures that would be
affected by the mittens' dirty work; humans would pay a
price too.

But Joey had a stern look on her face. I know that
look. It means the truth meter inside her head was
going haywire. Boing! Boing! Boing!

"Did you write that report yourself?" she asked
Margaux.

Again, Margaux gave what was fast becoming her
signature look: the caught-in-the-headlights look.

Margaux shrugged. "My mom helped me a little."

Joey didn't look convinced. "A little or a lot?"

"A . . . little." Margaux looked like she might cry.

Joey was unconcerned. "Really? Because
'compromised the structural integrity,' for example,
doesn't sound like something a kid, even a Science Squad
kid, would say."

And that was when Margaux burst into tears.

"My mom helped. She said wanted to make sure I get into your club and earn community service credits," *Margaux explained. "But I added the part about New York."*

At that point, Joey had her arm around Margaux. *"You should have just told us that you couldn't do the research that fast. Ned shouldn't have forced you."*

Joey turned to glare at ME!

Forced her? Puh-lease.

The leader always gets blamed for stuff. I didn't want Margaux to think I was a tyrant, so I tried to change the subject.

"Why don't we see about setting up your profile on the Science Squad HQ website?" I asked Margaux cheerfully.

Here's what she wrote: "Margaux Duval, age twelve. Just moved to the Eastern Shore from the Midwest. I'm interested in crafting and scrapbooking. And, of course, in saving the environment. I spell my name the French way because I was named for my great-grandmother, who lived in Paris for a whole year."

It was all I could do to not roll my eyes. On my mother's side are ancestors from the Pocomoke Nation, and on my dad's side are Accohannock Indians. I think that's pretty cool, but I don't say that on my profile page!

Margaux wanted to cram even more information onto her profile page. Like that her mom works for a big hotel chain setting up new openings and is holding her back a year in school because they move around so much. TMI.

My contribution to the conversation was to tell Margaux that she doesn't need to put anything about her mom on her profile, or about repeating sixth grade. I said it should be more about her science interests and accomplishments.

She didn't listen to me. What's the point of being the leader when no one does what you say?

While she finished up her profile, I checked the Mitten Watch website. There were no new sightings on the website. Are there ever going to be?

Papering the Town Blue

After two days of rain, I woke up this morning to the sun shining. Time to pass out more fliers. And this time we had our "Free Help" ads to share too!

We talked about things like erosion, damage to levees, and clogged water systems as we handed out our "Wanted" fliers. People were really receptive to us!

Next, we intercepted boaters on the docks and handed them our "Free Help" ads. A lot of them were skeptical. Some fishers told us we'd just get in the way. Others were convinced it was a scam to sell them wrapping paper, frozen pizzas, or chocolate bars, and didn't seem to believe us when we said we just wanted to check their gear for mittens.

We did get some customers, though, and Joey, Dante, and I worked hard to search their hauls. We didn't uncover a single mitten, just lots of blue crabs.

Margaux decided her job should be to watch Dooley. I don't think she liked the idea of digging through buckets of live crabs or that she could get pinched.

Dooley seemed to behave himself for Margaux. Although I think she might have been slipping him expensive hotel appetizers all afternoon.

Note to self: Remind Dante to stock up on dog poop bags.

Reunion with Elmer!

We met at 9:00 this morning to pass out more fliers. I was decidedly less enthusiastic to "raise awareness" today than yesterday. Dante must have been too. As we were about to set off, he stopped in his tracks and stamped his foot.

"Anybody else tired of walking around handing out brochures and talking with people?" he asked. "We're supposed to be mitten trackers, so let's go track them."

Dante was right. While we were definitely earning research and education stickers, we were also collecting pain and suffering stickers (if you count Band-Aids on your feet to cover blisters as stickers!).

Dr. Mo kept stressing how important it was to give out information, day after day, but it wasn't the most exciting assignment in the world. That's sort of true when you're hunting for arrowheads. You can search for a long time and sift through all kinds of muddy debris before you actually find one. It's meticulous* work.

Dante's defiance inspired me. I decided it was time to change tactics. I suggested that we go to the marina today and do some tracking. Then I added that I thought it would be awesome if we were the ones to find the mittens first, because if we were, we might be able to get a special First-to-Find badge!

Dante and Joey loved both ideas. Margaux did too. "I agree about the special badge," she said. "Do you think headquarters would let us design it? I could sketch out some ideas."

We all told her that was a great idea. But then she kept talking. "And even if we aren't first, we could get trophies that say we are. One time, when I didn't get first place in a Halloween contest—even though my Parisian artist costume was the best—my mom had a first-place trophy made especially for me."

Oh brother!

---

*Meticulous: Showing great attention to detail, even when it involves painstaking effort.

We agreed to meet at the fishing pier at the marina in thirty minutes. That gave us plenty of time to run home and get our crabbing nets, the kind that have long handles.

I raced home to grab my stuff. On my way there, I got a text from Mom: "Here's a way to make up for your poor choices yesterday. Dad's discovered stinkbugs on his crops in the south field. He needs you to pick them off as soon as possible. Love, Mom." Thanks for signing your name in your text, Mom.

But really? Stinkbugs. Ugh. My dad doesn't like to use insecticides, so this happens every season. Invasion of the vegetable-chomping insects. I thought my punishment should be to clean my room or something that my mom's been nagging me to do, not this.

I ignored the text and hurried back to meet the Squad.

Dante and I got to the marina about the same time. We looked around. Joey and Margaux weren't there yet, but guess who was: ELMER!

At first, we weren't sure it was Elmer. Could've been any twelve-year-old boy dangling his feet over the side of the pier. But his New York Mets baseball cap was a

major giveaway. Same one he wore last year. "Buenos dias, amigos!" he called out. "My dad finally got his visa! I was worried I was going to miss the whole summer! I biked over here right away to tell you the good news."

"How'd you know where to find us?" Dante asked.

"I didn't," Elmer confessed. "But it was such a nice day, I had a hunch it might be this place."

Joey and Margaux arrived ten minutes late. They'd gone to get crabbing nets that the hotel lends to guests. Joey screamed when she saw Elmer and gave him a big hug.

Margaux stood a little far from the group and awkwardly introduced herself. She even spelled out her name.

"It's French, right?" Elmer asked. He really knows how to turn on the charm!

Margaux blushed and nodded.

We decided to eat lunch first. Joey and Margaux had brought hotel sandwiches, and we dived right in. We figured we needed energy for crabbing. As we ate, a bunch of gulls kept dive-bombing us. One of them pooped right on Margaux's arm!

Dante and I laughed our heads off, but Elmer, always the "gentleman" (at least, that's what my mom says), jumped up and showed her where she could hose off. Dante and I started secretly calling Margaux "Margoo."

For hours, we hung over the side of the pier and used our nets to dredge up stuff in the water and around the pilings. There was a lot of seaweed and slimy stuff, besides soggy food wrappers and rotting orange peels.

Margoo found a ladies' purple sandal. "I'm going to keep it," she said. "I'll turn it into a decoration."

There were also some tiny white crabs and some broken crab claws and legs. Joey says that's not too upsetting, because crabs can regrow their limbs. Whoa!

Boaters aren't supposed to dump their trash in the water, but the only logical conclusion is that not everyone obeys the law. We even caught plastic straws in our nets. Ugh! So bad for fish! We tossed the little crabs back into the water and took the flotsam and jetsam* to the garbage cans by the marina's snack bar. There were a lot of gulls hanging around the cans. One of them made off with something, claws dangling, that

---

*I just learned what "flotsam" and "jetsam" mean. Each word has a specific meaning under maritime law. Flotsam is debris in the water that was not deliberately thrown overboard, like from a shipwreck or an accident. Jetsam is debris that was deliberately thrown overboard by the crew of a ship, most often to lighten the ship's load. Flotsam may be claimed by the original owner. Jetsam may be claimed by whoever discovers it.

could have been a mitten, but the gull flew up the bay and disappeared from sight.

"We should always bring binoculars with us when we're working," Joey suggested. "So we can spot things in the distance."

Lucky for me, heavy rains and thunderstorms are forecast tonight. Hopefully, that will get me off the hook for stinkbug stalking. (I told my mom I didn't get her text because I was so busy with Squad stuff today. I'm not sure she bought it.) Maybe the storms will wash the stinkbugs away!

All About Watermen

Today, Joey arranged for her parents to invite us on board their boat to inspect their crab pots for mittens. We didn't find any, but Margoo, at least, learned a lot.

"What exactly is a waterman?" she asked as we headed down to the docks. "Is it just another name for a fisherman?"

"Around here," Joey explained, "it means someone who works for himself or herself on the Chesapeake Bay fishing independently, not working for a big company. Watermen make their living by harvesting blue crabs, finfish, and oysters."

Joey's parents put us to work inspecting their dozens of crab pots for signs of mittens.

"It must be so beautiful being out on the bay all day," Margoo said. She certainly loves to chit chat.

"It is beautiful, that's for sure," Mrs. Holland agreed, "especially in the morning as the sun comes up—when the sky turns pink, purple, and gold. I never get tired of seeing it. But we do get pretty busy and work pretty hard."

"At least when you're working hard you're not cooped up in an office or a hotel," Margoo said.

"Or a classroom," Dante added.

"You've hit on one of the reasons we keep doing it," Mr. Holland said. "We're our own bosses. There's a great sense of freedom being out here on the open water."

"Do you make a lot of money?" Margoo asked.

Mr. and Mrs. Holland looked at each other and laughed. "We definitely don't do it for the money," Mr. Holland said. "We do it because of the natural beauty, the freedom, and one other reason—the tradition. Both our families have been watermen for generations."

Margoo was about to ask another question when Mr. Holland stood up and herded us off the boat.

"Okay, kiddos," he said. "Thanks for your help, but we need to get over to the marina to buy some paint for our crab pots."

"That's so they won't get eroded from the pollution in the bay, right, Pops?" Joey asked.

"Right, you are. That's my girl. You make good choices the rest of the day, you hear?" he said.

Mrs. Holland added, "Your dad and I are running the Waterman Legacy tour tonight, so we'll leave leftovers in the fridge if we somehow miss each other." Then she kissed Joey on top of the head.

"Who takes care of you when your parents aren't around?" Margoo asked once they were off the boat. She was so nosy.

Joey thought for a moment. "Everybody, I guess. Where we live, everyone is part of a big extended family. There's always someone looking out for me—grandmas, aunts, cousins."

"That's so cool," Margoo said. "It's just me and my mom looking out for each other."

Margoo was holding on to the waterman topic like she had claws. "Do your parents crab all year long?"

Joey shook her head. "Only April 1 to December 15."

"Then in the winter, they spend more time with you?"

"In the winter they dredge for oysters, but my dad says there are fewer and fewer oysters in the bay too. If you want to learn more about watermen, I'll take you on one of the legacy tours."

"That sounds really interesting," Margoo gushed.

And you know what else was interesting? Looking for mittens. I get that Margoo was new here and wanted to know more about the watermen and blue crabs, but I wanted to get back to hunting mittens. I wanted to yell, "Can we wrap this up, people?!" But I kept my cool.

After Joey's parents left, we hung out at the marina, looking for more work. Dante yelled, "Free help! Come get your free help!" And he waved our ads in the air. Not many takers and (obviously) no mittens. We're helping to raise awareness though. At least, that's what we keep reminding ourselves.

Just before we left, Dr. Mo texted that they're scheduled to moor Baywatch at the marina on Friday. She wants us to stop by to check in with her on our progress!

Catching Up with Dr. Mo

When Dr. Mo and her staff pulled into the marina today, Joey jumped up and down so much I was afraid the dock was going to collapse under our feet. Going aboard a research vessel makes me feel like a real scientist.

I called out to Dr. Mo, "We have lots to tell you and lots more questions!" We'd come up with five major questions at our last Science Squad meeting.

"I figured you would," she said. She invited us on board, handed us each a bottle of cold water, and took one for herself.

Elmer introduced himself and shook her hand.

"Well, welcome aboard Elmer Delcid," she said. Then she invited us to sit under the canopy, because it was a pretty sunny day.

We told her about our "Free Help" ads and our mitten search at the marina, where we found just about everything except mitten crabs.

"I'll bet you saw a lot of living organisms lurking down there under the pilings, though, right? Tiny invertebrates, plankton?"

"What's plankton?" Margoo asked.

"Plankton is a general term for plants, animals, and bacteria that float around in the water, carried by tides and currents," Dr. Mo said. "Some are small, and some can't even be seen with the naked eye. But trust me, they're definitely there."

"If you can't see them, how do you know they're there?" Margoo asked. Again with the questions. Obviously, she has a lot to learn about science.

"Look at samples under a microscope, maybe?" I offered.

"Exactly," Dr. Mo said. Then she went on to tell us about a cool project. Scientists are lowering special tiles underneath docks and letting the kinds of organisms that she was telling us about collect on the tiles for about three months. Some of the organisms are harmless, she said, but some turn out to be invasive species.

"Taken together, they're called a 'fouling community,'" she explained. "The first step is to identify what kinds of organisms are growing on the tiles."

I asked her why they just hang out around pilings. Turns out, they don't. They also attach themselves to boat hulls. She said that's why boaters need to make sure they thoroughly clean their hulls, especially below the waterline, before they move on to another body of water. Invasive species can move from bay to bay on small boats, just like they can hitchhike on large ships.

I was kind of bummed when she told us that, because our "Free Help" ad could have said that we clean boat bottoms, not just crab pots.

When I mentioned that, Dr. Mo said she had "misgivings" about us cleaning the bottoms of boats, which involves high-pressure hoses and very hot water. "It's best you leave bottom cleaning to the boat owners," she warned.

Dante howled with laughter at the idea of "bottom cleaning." Guess that's because one of his sisters is still in diapers. Sometimes, he can be sooo immature.

Margoo wanted to know if the tiles were decorator tiles. Thank you, Margoo, for getting us back to your interests. Again.

Dr. Mo laughed and said the tiles she was talking about are plastic and pretty plain looking, but they do important work.

Joey asked if we could do some of the work with tiles.

Dr. Mo said at some point her lab plans to distribute tiles to citizen scientists who are interested in studying invasive species. Volunteers will learn how to photograph and identify what they find on their tiles and how to send the results to the lab. She said she'd "keep us posted."

I hope she does, because that sounds like cool work. Much cooler than, say, picking bugs off beans on your family farm.

"In the meantime, should we keep looking around the docks for mittens?" I asked.

"It certainly doesn't hurt to look everywhere for them," she said, "but if you have access to a boat, you could also look in fresh water. You might see juveniles walking up streams, looking for places to eventually settle in for a few years."

At that moment, Joey's and Dante's eyes shot over to look at me.

"Where's your dad's canoe that you promised?" Dante asked.

I'm sure my face turned red at that. I hadn't actually asked my dad if we could borrow his canoe. I wasn't sure he'd be willing to let us use it, especially since I'd been kind of lax lately helping with the farm work. I needed to stall for time until I could get back on Dad's good side. That won't be easy unless I get out into those fields this weekend.

"R–r–right, my d–d–dad's canoe," I stammered. "I guess I'm a little concerned about the work involved in doing that. It can be hard work to canoe upstream. Before we do that, let's make sure we cover all the areas closer to home. I propose we go to the wetlands sanctuary first." The sanctuary is one of my favorite places. There are more than 300 acres of tidal wetlands. I've seen all kinds of crabs there.

Dr. Mo said my plan sounded reasonable. I'm not sure if she realized it, but she covered for me!

Wanting to change the subject, I jumped right into the first question we had for Dr. Mo: Exactly why can't people eat mittens? I'd meant to research that, but I got distracted by what I discovered online about an awesome new excavation site in Maryland. Archaeologists found tons of arrowheads and other stuff. Maybe I shouldn't have changed the subject after all . . .

Dr. Mo smiled and said she thought since we are such great researchers that we would already know the answers to that question. Joey glared at me, and Dante looked smug.

"For now," she said, "we want people to freeze mittens, rather than eat them, and get them to us. Later, if there's an outbreak and we want to control the population, then we might encourage people to eat them. However, it's not likely."

Then she went on to say that mittens aren't purists when it comes to their environment. They'll hang out in polluted water and can absorb heavy metals like mercury, lead, and cadmium, as well as hazardous chemicals, into their tissues. Which, of course, aren't good to consume.

"Then why do people eat them in Asia?" I asked. I wanted to establish that I did know some things!

She said that in those cultures, mittens are often grown in controlled environments like aquafarms. Why hadn't I come across that in my research? That would have been dynamite info for my presentation.

"You know what, Dr. Mo?" I said. "So many people are asking us if they can eat them, your research lab ought to make up another flier just about why everyone shouldn't eat mittens."

She looked surprised. "You know what, Ned? That's a great idea." Gold star for Ned Bolling!

Dr. Mo continued with another reason you shouldn't eat them: "Mittens can also carry parasites that cause lung problems."

Yikes!

Note to self: Warn Mom about this. She treats lots of patients, like kids with asthma, who have lung problems. People showing up with lung problems could be eating the meat in mitten claws! It's not likely, I guess, but as Joey's always saying, in the hunt for mittens we shouldn't leave any stone unturned.

As our vigilant timekeeper, Joey reminded me we had more questions for Dr. Mo. So I asked why mittens have "mittens." Elmer joked that a lot of kids think the hairy claws are to keep them warm in winter. We couldn't find an answer in our research.

Dr. Mo explained that no one really knows for sure (ah ha!), but probably the unusual patches were developed as a survival mechanism in their native environment. They may help them to get around somehow, she said, but they also have those eight sharp-tipped legs for that.

Joey wanted to confirm that both males and females have hairy claws. "They do," Dr. Mo said. "The tips of the claws are white in both sexes, but the patches cover more of the claws in the males."

"That just figures," Joey said. "Just like male birds. The males are showier."

Dr. Mo said she had time for one more question.

We had two more questions, but we settled on one about a crab jubilee. Joey asked, "Could the mittens have a crab jubilee, just like the blue crabs, if they didn't get enough oxygen?"

"Yes," Dr. Mo said, "but one thing about mittens is that they can survive for days outside water. For an aquatic crab, that's pretty unusual."

She went on to say that areas of little or no oxygen are called "dead zones," and scientists are working to reduce them.

"Just one more question, pretty please," Margoo said, and she put her hands together as if in prayer.

"We have to move when the tides are right, kids," Dr. Mo said. She stood to start packing stuff up. "One more question, but make it a quick one."

"Do mittens molt?"

Dr. Mo nodded her head. "Yes, about eighteen times during their life, according to Chinese scientists. That's all, folks! Email me your other questions."

As we walked away from the marina, we couldn't stop chatting about what we had learned. Margoo invited us to the Poolside Café again for lunch, gratis*. I wonder if her mom knows about all these free lunches?

---

*gratis: free

Preparing for the Wetlands

Our trip to the wetlands is tomorrow, so we focused on getting ready today.

We checked the tide tables and weather. Obviously, we want to go at low tide, which is better for sloshing around and seeing stuff. So we're going mid-morning.

Dante says he's bringing Dooley. Dooley usually spells trouble, especially if we're near marshes. He lives to dash into the water and chase after ducks. But I know I'm not going to be able to talk Dante out of bringing him.

I made a checklist as we talked to be sure I didn't forget anything.

Checklist:

- Wear boots. I'm hoping Joey will stress this to Margoo. So far, she's only been wearing these little shoes—Joey calls them "flats"—when we walk around town. If Margoo wears those to the wetlands, it will be disastrous.

- Wear a long-sleeve shirt and a hat. Even though it will be hot, these are an absolute must for bug and sun protection.
- Bring gear. We're all going to round up crabbing nets and buckets and gloves. And Elmer will bring a pair of binoculars.
- Bring cell phone. This is so we can take pictures (which is good, because sometimes the service is spotty out there). Margoo has a tablet, so she's going to bring that.
- Bring water and lunch. Actually, Margoo is going to bring us all boxed lunches. They're usually reserved for hotel guests, but she can get some for us. They each come with a water and a big chocolate chip cookie.
- Bring sunscreen and bug spray. I don't like blasting the wetlands with bug spray, but if our protective clothing isn't cutting it, we need a backup.

I think we're ready for tomorrow's "safari" (Dante's word for our adventure). I think it's going to be great!

Wetlands, Day 1

Poor Margoo.

We had agreed to meet at the entrance to the sanctuary this morning. She was the last of us to arrive, and when Dooley saw her, he got so excited that he jumped on her and got mud all over her white pants.

"Who wears white pants to go wading in muck?" I whispered to Joey.

"They aren't pants," Joey snapped. "They're leggings. She looks very sophisticated."

Whatever. At least she was wearing boots.

Along the first path we took, we spotted a couple of kayakers in the distance and heard some faraway voices. Human voices. There are always bird and animal noises— splashing, flapping, rustling, croaking, chirping. There could be dozens of people here, and we would never see them except as specks on the horizon.

The wetlands have been my favorite place since I was a kid. Some of my best memories are coming here with my mom and dad to look for wading birds like blue herons, white egrets, and glossy ibis with green-and-purple plumage—and for ducks like blue-winged and green-winged teals.

"This isn't as great as the state park," Dante said. "If we had a canoe, we could go on all the marked water trails." He shot a look at me. I chose to ignore it.

"Those are for tourists," I said, "not Eastern Shore locals like us. Now, let's go earn an observation sticker."

Margoo seemed to recover from the Dooley incident when she saw all the flowers. She flitted like a butterfly from cardinal flowers to blazing stars to rose mallows, taking photos and asking us their names. She gushed about how beautiful they all were, and Joey gushed back that she thought so too.

I thought it would be educational for Margoo to look at my favorite—arrow arum. I scooped up some of the leaves that were floating in shallow water and pointed out how they're shaped like arrowheads.

"You just like them because you collect arrowheads," Dante said to me. Then he motioned Margoo over to look at a clump of cattails.

"If your mom won't let you have a real pet," he said to her, "you could grow one of these in a pot."

Margoo gave Dante a withering look. Do all girls know how to do this look, or did she learn it from Joey?

Elmer spotted a crab. It wasn't a mitten (it was a fiddler), but at least it was a crab. The crab wasn't alone either. There was a whole posse of them just lying around in the mud.

Dante tried to explain them to Margoo, but she said she already knew about them. She then pointed to their distinct large claw as if she was saying "Duh."

Too bad, Dante. A missed opportunity to impress.

"They are my favorite because I play the fiddle," Margoo said.

"Me too!" Joey exclaimed. They both started jumping up and down and squealing. Girls are so weird sometimes. I had to make them stop.

"If we're quiet, we might see some birds," I said. (Is there a sticker for diplomacy?)

"Sorry," Joey whispered. "I think there might be a great blue heron right over there." She borrowed Elmer's binoculars and trained them on some nearby marshes, and just then one heron took off with a big flapping whoosh and flew right over us. It was probably looking for a more peaceful place.

Margoo asked me how we knew what it was. "All I saw was two very long legs and a flash of blue," she said.

Long legs, long bills, long necks—I told her that was the shorthand way of identifying wading birds.

"Do they fly south when it gets cold?" she wanted to know.

"Nope. They live here all year," Joey told her. "But there are some migratory birds that stop here in winter on their way south, Marg."

Marg? When did Joey start calling Margoo "Marg"?

That's when I heard a lot of thrashing around in the bushes. I thought maybe it was a muskrat or a sika deer. It was a wild animal all right—Dooley! He must not have been happy just chasing after ducks. He was on the hunt for snacks, human snacks.

We all ran to check out the commotion and found him scarfing down sandwiches and cookies. He even ate the wrappers! He had rummaged through two backpacks, Joey's and mine, by the time we heard him, and had helped himself to our lunches. He didn't bother with the water bottles, but everything else was totally chewed on or chewed up. He even tore apart the cardboard boxes.

"BAD DOG!" I yelled at Dooley. Dooley just wagged his tail and tried to give me slurpy dog kisses.

"He tears things up when he gets nervous," Dante tried to explain.

"You've got to get that dog more intense training," Joey scolded.

We shared the remaining lunches, then started for home.

When we were walking back, Margoo asked me if I really collect arrowheads and if she could come over to my house to see them sometime. I was surprised. I didn't think she'd be interested in weapon parts. Maybe she likes to collect things too?

I said sure but was elusive (like a mitten crab) on giving her a date. I had to think about that.

Tomorrow, we're going back to the wetlands sanctuary, because that's what everyone wants to do.

Wetlands, Day 2

For today's adventure, we each packed our own lunch and took turns keeping an eye on Dooley.

Margoo was still on a flower kick and, according to Joey, was planning some kind of wetlands arts-and-crafts project. Today, Margoo was dressed in all purple, except for giant dream-catcher earrings. At least she had switched to black pants. She complained that her white pants leggings were still a mess and she may never be able to get the stains out. If she keeps sticking her nose in flowers, she's going to have a bigger problem than paw prints on her leggings! She could get stung by a bee searching for nectar.

It wasn't long before she was nose deep in flowers again. She was inspecting a spotted flower closely when, before she could even ask, Dante told her it was joe-pye weed.

"Isn't that a hilarious name?" he asked. "It's a perennial plant that blooms in mid- to late summer." Clearly, Dante had been doing some research.

"And this one with the pretty spikey flowers?"

"That one's called purple loosestrife," I jumped in before know-it-all Dante could. "It's pretty, but it's an invasive plant."

Before we could stop her, Margoo started pulling it up. She grabbed a whole clump and started shaking it. "You guys pitch in. There's a lot of it here," she said.

"Um, definitely not a great idea, Marg," Joey said. "Plants can be hitchhikers, too, like the mittens. They can spread their seeds or pollen to other places."

Joey was right—we could have even carried that stuff on our clothes when we left. And who knew what Dooley had rolled around in already today. I figured the best thing we could do was take pictures of how much there was and its location, and report our findings to the sanctuary staff.

Margoo looked like she was going to cry. She said she was upset because she thinks she's seen purple loosestrife around the hotel grounds. She said her mom wanted to make sure the gardeners planted a lot of wildflowers for a natural look. I think she should definitely find out what her mom had her gardeners plant now that she knows about noninvasive perennials like cardinal flower, blazing star, and joe-pye weed.

Note to self: Print out a list of noninvasive perennials that Margoo can give her mom.

I really wanted to stop talking about flowers. I like flowers well enough, but we're supposed to be focusing on CHINESE MITTEN CRABS.

"Look over there," I said, trying to divert her attention.

Margoo squinted and said she didn't see anything. Maybe she needs glasses because a diamondback terrapin was sunning itself on some matted cordgrass three feet in front of her.

"I think the diamond-shaped rings covering its shell are so cool," Elmer said. I'm not sure where he came from.

Margoo didn't want to take a closer look, but Dooley sure did! He galloped over to investigate, and the diamondback pulled its head back into its shell.

I had pretty much given up trying to pry Margoo away from flowers and was poking around in some marshes when she started shouting. "Come quick! I found some mittens!" She was scooping up a bunch of squirmy brown things.

We all ran over to see. "Good guess," I said, peering into Margoo's net, "but those are marsh crabs."

I have to admit, marsh crabs do look a lot like the pictures I've seen of the mittens. They have a square carapace and are sort of the same color, but they're smaller and don't have a notch between their eyes or furry claws.

One thing marsh crabs do have in common with mittens is burrows. In fact, when we dumped them out of the net, some of them scurried right back into theirs.

When they were out of sight, I heard the telltale rapping sound. The males make rapping sounds when they want to defend their burrows.

I was going to point it out to Margoo, but she was more interested in flowers than burrows.

"Hey, Margaux!" Dante called. "There are periwinkles over there." He pointed to a clump of tall grass.

"Oooh, I love periwinkles," she said, making her way toward them. Before I could stop her, she plucked off a bunch of what she thought were flowers. Really, they were little snails. After she got a close look at them, she threw them down and squealed.

Dante thought it was hysterical. "They're alive! They're alive!" he shrieked like he was in a horror movie.

"They won't bite," I told a horrified Margoo. "There are all kinds of snails and worms in the mud here."

Let me make this perfectly clear: Dante didn't actually lie to Margoo. What he was pointing to were marsh periwinkles. They do look like flower buds from a distance, but they're not. The snails hang on to tall stalks of grass to escape predators like mud crabs. But the snails are grayish-white or tan. Real periwinkle flowers are blue, and I would have thought Margoo would have noticed that.

Dooley took Margoo's tossing of the "flowers" as an invitation to play. He jumped and barked and raced around in circles, rolled over and over in the mud and grass, and then plopped down right on our backpacks and drooled all over them. (Maybe he should have been named Drooley!)

Note to self: *Remind everyone to check for deer ticks. They can be really bad in summer. Dante should check Dooley too. It's especially hard to find ticks on squirmy dark-colored dogs.*

After all THAT, the entire Squad was considerably less enthusiastic to continue our search for mittens.

We decided we'd try again one more time tomorrow. Even though I'm getting a little bored of the wetlands (I'm not sure we're going to find anything!), I don't mind going back again, because it buys me time to get on Dad's good side so I can negotiate about the canoe.

Anyway, when I got home I found a list of "good" perennials online and printed a copy for Margoo. And then I sent my purple loosestrife shots to the sanctuary.

Good deeds for the day—done.

Wetlands, Day 3

I don't know what's gotten into Joey lately, but she continues to act really funny. Take, for instance, today when I was talking about green tree frogs, which she used to think were interesting. Out of nowhere, Margoo said, "Yeah and if you kiss one, he might turn into a prince."

Um, okay. Not sure where she was going with that. But Joey doubled over like it was the funniest thing she'd ever heard. Girls are so weird sometimes. I feel like I've been saying that a lot lately . . .

Elmer and I exchanged eye rolls, and I talked on and on about other kinds of frogs, which I think is a really interesting topic.

"You really know a lot about nature, Ned," Margoo said.

I thought she was being sarcastic, but that didn't stop Dante from trying to one-up me (as usual). He piped up with "I know just as much as he does. This, for example, is the northern water snake." And he held the writhing snake out, two inches from Margoo's face, with both hands.

Guess what? Margoo screamed and backed away. Dante gently put the snake back on the ground but seemed oblivious to Margoo's discomfort, because he continued his little talk. "It's a nonvenomous aquatic snake that lives in lakes, swamps, streams, and other waterways throughout the Chesapeake Bay watershed." Now he was sounding like a dork.

"Dante, dude, what's with you?" Elmer asked.

A rustling noise in the grasses saved us all from Dante's presentation. A nutria, a big brown rodent that lives in the wetlands, popped out to say hello. They're an invasive species that's been nearly wiped out here, so it was wild to see one. Before we could explain what it was to Margoo (or take a picture), she screamed, "RAT!" Then she started running back down the trail. Joey went flying after her. Once Margoo was sure the "rat" was gone, she agree to come back to the group.

As we slogged along after that, I decided to step in as the leader of the Squad. I reminded everyone, Margoo especially, that we were scientists looking for mittens, and we needed to keep our cool, even when rat-like creatures jumped out at us from nowhere.

Things quieted down for a while, until Elmer asked, "Ned, remember that carving your dad made for me of a redhead?"

"You like redheads?!" Margoo shouted. Did I mention that she has red hair? She and Joey were at it again, squealing and carrying on. Joey has been acting, well, unprofessional since she started hanging out with Margoo. She used to be serious about science.

Elmer rolled his eyes. "The redhead is a duck that stops at the Chesapeake Bay on its way to Texas and Mexico."

Because of the ridiculous redhead distraction, we almost stepped on a spotted turtle sitting in the middle of a path.

"Are those yellow spots real, Ned?" Margoo asked. "They look too bright to be real."

"Oh, they're very real," Dante answered before I could.

"I'm going to ask my mother if I can keep this one as a pet," she said as she bent down to pick it up.

"Stop!" Joey yelled. "It's a threatened species."
Maybe the old Joey was back!

We might have stayed there longer, taking
photographs and snooping around. But Dooley spotted
an American black duck tipping its head into a little
pond. Of course, he went galloping through grasses and
mud, barking like crazy and slipping and sliding, trying to
catch it.

Mission not accomplished. Luckily, Dooley isn't as
great at catching ducks as he is at chasing them. When
he came back, he shook himself off the way dogs do and
splattered water all over us.

We were all mad at Dante for still not being able
to get Dooley to sit and stay when he sees a duck, but
Dante says when a Chessie sees a waterfowl, he goes
for it. And if you can believe it, Dante was mad at me.

I was so tired when I got home. But a message
from the sanctuary's environmental manager got me
energized again. He thanked me for the photos and said
purple loosestrife grows fast and can crowd out native
wetland plants pretty quickly, and that they'll monitor
it. Another gold star for me! It's great to feel like I'm
really making a difference.

Joey on the Case

Today, Joey threw the Squad a switcheroo. She informed us that instead of handing out fliers or looking for mittens, we were visiting a cargo shipping business. She wanted to interview someone in charge at the facility to find out if they are following the latest ballast water regulations. Yawn. She said the place was near us, but it wasn't. It took TWO buses to get there! My parents probably wouldn't like it if they knew I was traveling so far away.

"Come on. It'll be fun," she said. "It'll be nice to do something different for a change." Then she looked pointedly at me and added, "And a chance to sharpen your crime scene skills, Sherlock."

Um, okay. Sure, I like to read mysteries, but I'm not a Holmie or anything. Ha! Get it?

Anyway, I didn't appreciate her attempt at humor, so I asked, "Hey, Joey, can we wear disguises? Trench coats, big hats, mustaches?"

Joey just ignored me. Margoo thought it was funny though.

"What do they ship from there?" Dante asked.

"Liquid natural gas." Joey had clearly been planning this for a while.

"Great idea," Dante said sarcastically. "Investigate a company that ships gas, which weighs nothing and is flammable. Why don't we investigate a feather company? Maybe we could take THREE buses and find one in Delaware."

"You're just showing what an ignoramus you are!" Joey yelled. "LNG is not seriously flammable, and it must weigh something, because tankers carrying it have to have ballast water just like everyone else." By this point, they were so loud that some tourists had stopped to stare at them.

As always, Elmer was the voice of reason. "Wait, guys," he said. "Shouldn't we ask Dr. Mo's advice before going to this place on our own?"

Joey reminded us that the last time we saw Dr. Mo, she didn't have time to discuss investigating ballast water compliance.

I'm pretty sure Dr. Mo would have said it wasn't a job for kids and that the government is in charge of that kind of stuff. Then she would have given us the usual pep talk about making a valuable contribution by our campaigning and handing out fliers. I'm sure Joey thought of this, too, which is why she didn't run it by Dr. Mo to begin with.

"Come on," Joey said. "We're wasting time." And hustled us to the nearest bus stop.

We had school IDs, so we could ride for free at least. Well, everyone except Margoo, who didn't have an ID, at least not one from our school. "Not a problem," she told the driver and pulled a twenty-dollar bill out of her pink-and-purple backpack.

The driver sighed and pointed to the sign that says, "EXACT CHANGE ONLY." We were off to a great start. The rest of us managed to pull together enough change from our pockets and backpacks to pay for Margoo.

On the looooong bus ride, Joey updated us with her latest findings:

- Any ship that enters a US port and wants to discharge ballast water has to follow certain rules.

- *The old way was to dump out old water and suck up new water in the middle of the ocean.*
- *Now there's a better way: treat the ballast water with a system on board the ship.*
- *The system has to pass tests, and if it does, the coast guard will give your ship an official seal of approval.*

Joey really will make an excellent investigative reporter. She's obsessed with this compliance business.

When we finally got to the place, there was a ten-foot-high fence around it and a guard who sat reading the newspaper in a glass booth. Beyond the fence we could see these big white domes. Joey said she thought it might be where the gas was stored.

"What can I do for you?" the guard asked.

"We're here to see Mr. Reinholt, the chief technical officer," Joey said.

"Yes, I know who he is," the guard said. He was eyeing us suspiciously. I would have too, if I was in his shoes.

Then he asked if we had an appointment. I couldn't believe we would all go along on Joey's harebrained scheme—complete with two bus rides (!!)—without an appointment. But Joey surprised us all by saying that we did.

The guard made a phone call and said Mr. Reinholt would be down shortly.

I hoped that was true, because I really had to pee. And, thankfully, it was. He was a tall, older man wearing a hard hat. He shook all our hands and gave Joey an especially big smile.

"I'm very impressed with the questions you sent me," he said. "How did you get involved in ballast water issues?"

"We're members of the Eastern Shore Science Squad, Guardians of the Bay," Joey explained. "We got interested in ballast water issues because of our research on invasive species, specifically the Chinese mitten crab. We're hoping to get Invasive Species badges by the end of summer."

"Ah," he said. "I'm familiar with invasive species issues, but not about the . . . What did you call it? The 'Chinese mitten crab'?"

It was like we had choreographed our moves ahead of time. All five of us reached into our backpacks to pull out the fliers and the "Wanted: Dead or Alive" posters. I was fastest and handed the papers to him first. Ta da!

"My, my," he said. "You young scientists are well-prepared, I see. Thank you. I'll make sure to look these over." Then he motioned to Joey to follow him. "I've printed out the questions you sent me. How about if we all go into the cafeteria, and I'll do my best to answer them? For safety and security reasons, I can't take you into the rest of the buildings."

In the cafeteria, he took off his hard hat, bought us all drinks and ice cream, and showed us where the restrooms were. Then we got down to business.

"As to your main question, do we comply with ballast water treatment regulations, yes we do. But it's complicated, and the challenge for us is deciding what best suits our needs."

"Can you explain further?" Joey asked.

"We always want to choose the most cost-effective and appropriate solution for our vessels. Natural gas is challenging cargo for our crews."

"So, do you release your ballast water into the open ocean, or do you use onboard treatment systems?"

"There are now government regulations saying all companies must have an onboard treatment system, and there are several types to choose from."

Joey was furiously writing notes in her notepad. Man, she was serious about this thing.

Joey: "Do your ships carry the US Coast Guard's seal of approval?"

Mr. Reinholt: "We're working toward that goal. As I said, liquid natural gas is a challenging cargo."

Joey: "Why?"

Mr. Reinholt ignored her question and abruptly stood up. "I hope that answers your concerns," he said, taking a phone out of his pocket and scrolling through it. "I have a meeting now. I'm going to pass this information on to our employees about Chinese mitten crabs. Keep me posted on your quest."

Joey mumbled the whole way out about "evasion tactics." I don't think this is the last time Mr. Reinholt is going to hear from her!

We had plenty of time on the ride home to rehash our waste-of-time-except-for-the-ice-cream visit and decide what we were going to do next.

At one point, Dante said, "It's dumb we haven't found any mittens. We need to look upstream. Where's that canoe you promised, Ned?

"I'm working on it," I said and pretended to nod off.

Note to self: Ask Dad to borrow the canoe on Sunday—after I finish with the revolting stinkbug chore! Ugh. I can't believe I've spent the past two Saturdays prying stinkbugs off bean, pepper, and tomato plants. I'd rather be mitten crab—or arrowhead—hunting!

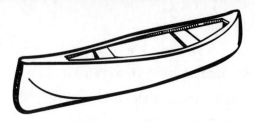

We've Got a Canoe!

Dad seemed happy with my stinkbug pickings yesterday, so I was ready to ask about the canoe after dinner. We had Chinese takeout. I took my fortune cookie message, which said, "It is not in your nature to give up," as a good sign for what I was about to do.

I was clearing the table like a good son (easy to do when you have takeout) and catching my dad up on the Squad's trips to the wetlands. He asked if we'd seen any wood ducks, which are his favorite.

"No, but we actually heard one, I think. You know that *hoo-w-eek* sound that you taught me to listen for? But I'm not sure because my friends were being kind of noisy. But when we got home, I sent them a little TED Talk about the male wood duck. And I told them how it has just about every color on itself, like green and purple patches and white stripes on its head, red eyes, a reddish-orange bill, and a reddish-brown body. And that it lives in the Chesapeake Bay region's freshwater wetlands and streams from spring through autumn. Everyone said they really want to look for one the next time we go to the wetlands."

I was full-on babbling. I tend to do that when I'm nervous. Clearly, my dad could sense something was up.

"Did you want to ask me something, son?" my dad interrupted. He was on to me.

"So, yes," I started. "Remember how I told you that Dr. Mo said a good place to look for Chinese mitten crabs was upstream?"

"I do," my dad said. Sometimes, he's so tired after working on the farm all day that it seems like he doesn't have the energy for much talking.

"Well, I think probably the best spot to look is where you and I used to go to find arrowheads, don't you agree?"

"Yes, that seems logical," my dad said, looking a little perplexed. "But where are you going with this?"

"Well, I think we probably need a canoe to do that." I gave him a cautious smile.

My dad put down his newspaper and fake swatted at me. He clearly knew where I was going with the conversation now.

I took that as a sign to continue on. "Well, we were wondering, the Science Squad was wondering, that is, if we could borrow your canoe for a bit."

"What's 'a bit'?" *my dad asked.*

"A week maybe?"

"How many of you?"

"Me, Dante, Joey, Elmer, and Margoo—I mean, Margaux."

"Who's that last one?"

"Margaux. M-a-r-g-a-u-x. She's new. Dante and I call her Margoo ever since a gull pooped on her arm."

"NED!" *My mom said as she came flying out of the laundry room.* "That's not nice!"

My mom thinks being nice is the most important thing in the world.

"We don't say it to her face, Mom. Just behind her back."

"That's even worse!"

Geez. Off topic!

"Anyway, Dad," *I said,* "I promise to take perfect care of your canoe. I know it's birchbark and was Grandpa Ned's. It's a family heirloom, I get that. But Joey and I are experienced paddlers, and the *others can just squish into the middle. It's not like we'll be carrying a lot of gear. And finding these crabs is important if we want to get our Invasive Species badges."*

"How are you going to get the canoe to water?"

I hadn't thought about that.

"If you want to do it tomorrow, we can put it onto the top of my van," Mom said. "I can drop you kids off at a designated spot on my way to work around eight in the morning and pick you up at four."

"I want you all to sign a contract," my dad said.

I groaned. My parents are big on responsibility contracts. But, of course, I said everyone would.

I've copied it onto the next page.

I _____ promise to treat Mr. Bolling's
(full name printed here)
canoe with care, to obey the rules of water safety, in
particular the rule to wear a life jacket at all times, and
to never stand up suddenly in the vessel. And I promise
to return the canoe in the condition in which I found it.
I understand that if I do not honor all aspects of this
contract, my borrowing privileges will be revoked.

Furthermore, I confirm that my parents are fully
aware of the risks inherent in canoeing and have given
their permission for me to ride in Mr. Bolling's vessel
without adult supervision.

Signed,

_____

I texted everyone that our first canoe trip is
tomorrow morning and that everyone AND THEIR
PARENTS (my dad insisted on this) needed to be at
my house by 7:30 to sign contracts. I printed out five
copies.

I hope everyone can make it.

Sleuthing Upstream

Everyone showed up on time this morning and signed the contracts. I gave them to my dad, and he meticulously helped my mom strap the canoe to the top of the van.

There are a lot of rivers and streams around our town that feed into the bay. I picked a stream that not many people know about, except for guys like me and my dad looking for arrowheads or other buried treasure. It's where I'd travel if I was a mitten on the run.

My mom dropped us off in a clearing near the stream, and we carried the canoe very carefully to the water's edge, carefully got in, and carefully paddled off.

It was all good for a while. We pulled the canoe up on shore and sloshed around in the shallow, slow-moving water, looking for mittens. Then we went downstream a little farther and pulled the canoe onto a shady place to have lunch before we set off again for more mitten tracking. That's when a dragonfly buzzed Margoo and

119

she freaked out. She jumped up, and the canoe wobbled a little. That made her act even more panicked, and she grabbed onto Joey. Then they both splashed into the water!

Elmer, Dante, and I couldn't stifle our laughter as we saw the girls soaking wet.

When we finally fished them out of the water, Margoo said her hair would be frizzy, like it was a major crisis. So she used MY PHONE and called her mom to come get her and Joey at the place where my mom dropped us off this morning. "We need to get into some fresh

clothes," she said to us boys. Then to Joey, she said, "We can hang out at the pool this afternoon."

I could have predicted Margoo bailing out, but Joey giving up a day on the water just because her clothes were soaking wet? That was a head-scratcher.

There was a small path that ran along the stream. Because we'd made a lot of stops and were paddling upstream, I didn't think the walk was going to be all that far. So the girls set off to meet Margoo's mom.

That left Dante, Elmer, and me to paddle farther upstream. And those two guys know zilch about paddling. I gave Elmer a quick lesson, and he did all right. Dante was a little miffed that I didn't pick him, but I said it was simply a matter of Elmer being older.

The water was so clear you could see straight down to the bottom. Dr. Mo had told us that juvenile mittens often go for smaller rivers and streams with slower-moving waters. We pulled the canoe on shore and tied it to a tree, another shady spot, and started our search.

"Look out, mittens, here we come, ready or not," Elmer said.

"Let's not forget to look on the banks, guys," I said. "Remember that mittens sometimes walk on land."

"Look at this mess over here," Elmer said. "Part of the bank looks like it's collapsed on top of itself like it's melted, and it has all kinds of little holes in it." He was poking with a tree branch at a clump of mud. It reminded me of when the tide comes in on the beach and washes over somebody's sandcastle that they took all day to build.

"Could be a burrow," I said. I reached for my phone to take a picture and realized it was probably sitting poolside at the Edgewater Grande Resort by then. Margoo must have put my phone in her pocket, because I totally forgot she had it.

I was so mad! I told the guys I was going a little farther upstream. I needed to cool off.

While I didn't find a mitten, I did find an arrowhead. As I was washing off my latest finding in the stream, I heard Elmer shout, "Ned, come quick!"

I wrapped the arrowhead in some leaves to protect it, shoved it in my pocket, and hurried to see what was going on. Elmer and Dante were swinging their nets through the water like crazy, first here, then there, trying to catch something that looked an awful lot like mitten crabs! There were at least a dozen of them, skittering in all directions.

"Quick! Take a picture!" Dante yelled.

"With what, my photographic memory?!" I shouted.

All that splashing around and net swinging brought up the mud from the stream bottom. That made it hard to see, and the crabs disappeared before we could capture any of them—like bank robbers in getaway cars.

After that fiasco, we hunkered down on the bank, pulled off our boots, and cooled our toes in the water.

"I'm dying of thirst," Dante said. "Do you think we could drink this water? Looks pretty unpolluted."

"Looks can be deceiving, my good man," I said. "There could be poisons in this water." We'd brought five bottles of water, and we'd guzzled them all down at lunch.

Guess what else we didn't have? A watch. Who needs one when you have a cell phone? We tried looking at the angle of the sun to decide if it was 5:00.

We weren't THAT far off, but my mom was pretty upset by the time we finally got there. When we lugged the canoe, which seemed much heavier going back, to the place where we were going to meet her, she was leaning against the van door, tapping her finger to her wrist. "Where have you been? I've been trying to call you. You're thirty minutes late," she said.

I told her how we lost my cell phone and ran out of water. I knew the water part would set off alarms. She has loads of scary emergency-room stories about people getting seriously dehydrated.

She grabbed some water out of her car and told us to sit down and drink right then and there. Then she started feeling our foreheads and taking our pulses. She asked us all kinds of questions, like were we dizzy, and had we been peeing, and did we drink any of the stream water, and what day was it.

I don't know how we got the canoe strapped to the car—superhuman Mom strength, I guess.

It wasn't until we scrambled into the car that she realized Joey and Margoo were missing. "Where are the girls?" she asked in a kind of panicky voice. We assured her that they were fine, but she still insisted on calling Margoo's mom to confirm that the girls had made it safely to the pool. Thank goodness she used her phone, since Margoo still had mine.

When we got home she immediately gave me the once-over . . . while my dad did the same for his canoe.

"I want you to keep drinking water," my mom said.

"Looks good," my dad said.

After I wolfed down dinner, I borrowed my mom's phone and called Dr. Mo to tell her we thought we saw mittens today, but they got away.

"They can be fast-moving little critters all right," she said. "And remember, if they were mittens, they could have been juveniles that were migrating even farther upstream, not just hiding under rocks or in burrows. Did you happen to notice if they had furry claws?"

I hadn't. How could I have not noticed?

"It's harder to detect juveniles because they are smaller, of course," she went on to say, "but also because they may not have any, or as much, setae on their claws. Upload your pictures, and I'll take a close look."

That's when I had to confess our humiliating no-phone disaster.

Dr. Mo was really nice about it. She pointed out that there are often setbacks in scientific investigations and that it "happens to the best of us." That made me feel a little better.

I think I'll go lounge in the hammock for the rest of the night. It's been a long day.

FOOLED!

Scratch that. No rest for the weary. Joey tricked me tonight, and I fell for it. Big time.

Just as I was settling into the hammock, she called our landline to tell me to come to Edgewater quickly. She said that she and Margoo found a mitten in the pool!

Okay, so seeing it written down makes it even more ridiculous that I was duped. Still, I hopped on my bike and raced over there, yelling to my parents on my way out the door.

Margoo and Joey were calmly stretched out on lounge chairs when I got there and acting weird.

Joey reached into a bag and pulled out this ugly red plastic toy shaped like a crab. "We bought it at the hotel gift shop," she said, dangling it in front of my eyes. She was laughing so hard she started to get the hiccups. "I can't believe you fell for it! How could a mitten end up in a chlorinated hotel pool?"

I was furious for falling for that stupid trick. I should have picked up on clues that it was a trap. To make it worse, I tried to defend myself. "Mittens can survive in all kinds of conditions. And they've been known to walk hundreds of miles over land, so it's conceivable one could end up in the pool." That made Joey snort-laugh.

I was not amused, so I grabbed my cell phone from Margoo and stormed away.

"Don't be so <u>crabby</u>!" Margoo called after me. That stupid pun got the girls laughing even more.

About ten minutes after I got home, I was upstairs in my room when I heard our landline ring. Then my mom yelled up to me that Joey was on the phone. WHAT?

"Tell her I'm asleep!" I called down.

That didn't fly with my mom, so I finally got on the phone. Joey wanted to apologize for the plastic crab trick. "I was a jerk," she said.

"You were," I said. "Not cool at all."

Joey asked if I could forgive her and if she could still go on the canoe trip tomorrow. I kind of needed her to come since my dad revoked Margoo's contract when he found out she was responsible for a breach of water safety, Dante has to babysit his sisters, and Elmer is going out of town to visit family. But I didn't need to tell her that.

Joey also said she'd even bring me some Smith Island cake that the hotel's chef had made special. The Smith Island cake is Maryland's official state dessert.

"I tried it," she said. "It tastes pretty authentic."

An authentic one has at least eight and sometimes twelve thin layers of cake and gooey chocolate icing. It's like an engineering masterpiece, besides being the best cake you ever tasted.

"Oh, so I get to eat the crumbs that you and your new best friend couldn't finish?" I asked. I'll admit it—I was in the mood to be dramatic. And my feelings were a little hurt that Joey spent all her time with Margoo now.

"C'mon Ned. I saved you a giant brand-new piece. And Margaux isn't so bad. But she's not my best friend. You are."

"Okay," I said. "Be at my house at 7:45 tomorrow, sharp. And bring the cake."

Intriguing Developments

Mom dropped Joey and I, and two gigantic slices of cake, off at the stream early this morning. It was fun hanging out with just me and her.

We started by paddling the canoe to the scene of yesterday's crab getaway and poked around again. This time I had my cell phone camera ready.

But it wasn't long before we took a break to eat.

"I wish we could set out traps for them," Joey said.

I told her that in Germany, they tried setting up traps near dams. But since mittens can move onto land to get around traps, it's difficult to catch them. The Germans have had a lot of practice trying to stop them. The mittens arrived in their country in the early 1900s. It's crazy to think that mittens have been outfoxing people for more than one hundred years!

"Let's ask Dr. Mo about it," I said. "Maybe we could build some traps ourselves and put them in places where the streams are narrow but the banks are steep."

"Remind me again what mittens eat?" Joey asked. She had icing all over her fingers and face. I think she knew the answer; she was just bored with trap talk.

"They aren't fussy eaters," I said. I told her they eat just about anything they can get their ~~hands~~ claws on. They go into spawning areas and eat the eggs of other species, like the blue crab. They gobble up algae, plants, fish carcasses, and small invertebrates. "Then they hunker down into their burrows to digest all that food."

I reminded Joey that they also compete with the blue crab for places to live. "The bay's pretty big, but if everyone's interested in the same prime real estate, then it could turn into a crustacean battleground."

"I'd like to see one of them try to take a blue crab," Joey said. "That's one of the ways they lose their body parts."

After that, we paddled farther upstream for hours, looking everywhere: the streambed, along banks . . .

"I have a feeling we're not going to find any mittens today," Joey said.

"We can't give up," I said. "They could be hiding in plain sight. The mittens are pretty much the same color as their environment. They have the perfect camouflage. We need to think like—"

Joey interrupted me to say she was getting tired of talking about mittens and did I know Dante had moved on from Margoo to a new girl he was trying to impress?

I was clueless! Dante was trying to impress Margoo? I guess that made sense . . .

Joey seemed oblivious to my ignorance. She said there was a girl with a beagle in the dog training class that Dante takes Dooley to. Joey and Margoo have seen them walking their dogs together all over town. I guess Dante's been giving this girl tips on getting her dog to be better behaved. The kid is only ten years old. I don't know why he's bothering with girls right now.

I asked Joey how she found all that out, and she just shrugged and said, "I'm an investigative reporter, remember?"

We were on time to meet my mom. After we dropped Joey off, my mom dragged me along to do some errands.

When we got home, I was shocked to see who was stretched out in MY hammock.

Ack—gotta run. My dad is calling me down for dinner. I'll pick this up later . . .

My Surprise Visitor

So, back to my surprise visitor. It was good ol'
Margoo! She said she wanted to apologize to my dad for
falling out of his canoe. My dad wasn't home, but that
didn't stop my mom from asking Margoo if she wanted to
come inside.

Mom must have missed the SOS looks I was shooting
at her. I mean, I wouldn't say Margoo and I are friends.
She's just so . . . different from me. Although, admittedly,
before today I hadn't taken the time to get to know
her.

Anyway, after my mom served us some of her
delicious mint iced tea in the kitchen, Margoo asked if I
could show her my arrowheads. "I heard you found a new
one," she said. Where do girls find out all this stuff?

Still, I was more than happy to show them to her. So
I told her I'd be right back and ran upstairs to get my
display cases.

"Here they all are," I said, lugging them to the table. To protect them from dust and oxygen exposure, I keep them in trays with glass tops. "This is my most valuable one," I said, pointing. "Experts think that indigenous peoples used Clovis points like this to hunt probably 10,000 years ago. See how sharp the point is on it?"

"That's amazing!" Margoo said. "Where did you find it?"

"On one of the islands in the bay. That's the best place to search for them."

"And what about these others?"

"Some of them are from streambeds and creeks near here, like the one I found when we were looking for mittens yesterday. They're all over the place if you know how to look. It's kind of like panning for gold, I guess. Most times when you find an arrowhead, you're the first one to touch it since the original owner. When you research what you find, you learn a lot about the people who used them, like how they lived. That's why I want to be an archaeologist."

Margoo seemed impressed, so I showed her another display case. "I found some of these on the farms around here. I even found these three on our farm."

"On farms and in streams, okay, but how do you know <u>exactly</u> where to find them?"

"You have to know what clues to look for and not give up if you don't find anything on your first try . . . just like us with the mittens." I explained that people needed a place to grow crops, plus a water source for themselves and to attract animals to hunt. So they looked for nice flat land with good soil and a couple of streams nearby.

I was on a roll. "You need a farmer's permission to go arrowhead digging on his farm, but my dad knows plenty of the farmers around here, so it's not a problem for me."

"Where's the arrowhead you found after I fell overboard?" Margoo asked. "I wish I could have been there."

"It's still in the sink in the basement. I haven't washed it off yet. You need to wash each arrowhead off with cold water and a little soap, using an old toothbrush to gently remove all the dirt. Did you notice how clean the arrowheads in my collection are?"

Margoo nodded. She seemed really impressed.

"You're probably also wondering how I keep track of them all. I assign them each a number and then catalog them in a notebook. I record the date, the type of material, and where I found it—say, in the southwest corner of the Jones's farm."

"Kind of like what we're supposed to do if we find a mitten—give Dr. Mo as many details as we can about its location."

"Exactly!" I said. You know, maybe Margoo isn't so bad after all.

Then we got to talking about other stuff. I guess it isn't just her and her mom. She has a brother in the army! She didn't say anything about her dad, and I didn't ask. It didn't seem like it was my business.

But she also asked all sorts of questions about our farm: how many acres it was and what kinds of vegetables we grow. I guess that's why I started telling her about how I spent two Saturdays in a row collecting stinkbugs.

I thought she'd be grossed out, but she said she actually thinks insects are interesting (as long as they're not flying right at you, I guess). She said that if I ever had to do stinkbug duty again, she'd love to tag along.

Then we got to talking about the Terra-Cotta Warriors and agreed it would be awesome to visit there someday.

Maybe I've been too hard on ~~Margoo~~ Margaux.

My mom asked Margaux if she'd like to stay for dinner. It was her way of saying it was time to wrap things up, and Margaux got the message.

"No thank you, Mrs. Bolling," Margaux said. "I'd better get going. See you soon, Ned. I'd love to talk more about colleting arrowheads sometime."

And, of course, my mom commented on Margaux's "nice manners" after she left.

There was only one awkward moment the whole afternoon. When I suggested we look for arrowheads together in the fall (when it wasn't so hot), she just nodded her head and looked away. That was when she started asking me about our farm. I'm not sure what that was about.

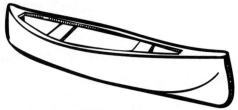

Need to Find
Special Guests. STAT!

Today, Dante, Elmer, and I took the canoe one last time. Joey said she had other stuff to do. I suspect she was hanging out with Margaux, who probably also had "stuff to do."

"I think she's spending too much time with Margaux," I said.

"Don't you mean Margoo?" Dante asked, chuckling. I just ignored him.

The three of us paddled along more streams and small rivers, searching for mittens. It would have taken the whole summer to explore them all. We were having a great time, despite not finding a single mitten. Dr. Mo keeps asking if we need more fliers, which I think is her way of saying that we need to refocus and get back to our raising awareness campaign.

We had a great time, in spite of not finding a single mitten. Well, at least I was having a great time until

Dante asked me about the special guests I said I'd invite to our mitten hunt, way back when I tried to convince him and Joey to agree to doing the mittens as our summer project. Man, Dante doesn't forget a THING.

"Plans are almost firmed up," I lied.

What am I going to do?!

Project in Peril

At today's Science Squad meeting, Joey said she had a serious announcement to make. She said she thought we should scrap the mitten project "while there's still half of summer left to patch together something more certain, like those dead zones Dr. Mo was talking about."

I was shocked. "I think we have a great project," I said. "We can't give up now. Remember that the Chinese mitten crab is listed as one of the worst invasive species in the world. It's in the top one hundred."

"Yeah, so what if they're in the top one hundred if there aren't any here?" Dante asked. "Then our project is in the top one hundred most embarrassing Science Squad projects ever." I have to wonder if Dante is losing interest because he wants to spend time with his new dog-walking pal.

He segued to his usual tirade about overdevelopment: "Maybe the special guests should be the city council, who could update us on hotel-caused pollution," he said. "I'd like to investigate that!"

Margaux spoke up and said that was unfair and insulting.

I ignored Dante's rantings and tried to calm everyone down. "Let's remember that scientific research is tedious, but it's very important. We're part of a community of scientists determining if the mittens are here right now or not. It's the first step, and a really important step, I might add."

I was way up on my "high horse" (as my dad would say). I continued, "My instincts tell me the mittens are out there. We just have to figure out where. And when they are found, thanks to our help, scientists can decide on how to get rid of them. If that's even possible . . ."

Elmer came to my defense. "I think Ned's right," he said. "We're doing important work. We're contributing to the pool of scientific knowledge on invasive species."

"Our project stands. This meeting is adjourned," I said. Even though I didn't want to admit it, I was just as frustrated as everyone else.

Later that afternoon, Margaux texted me from the pool. She wanted to know if I could show her some of the places I hunt for arrowheads this weekend. I'm not sure why she is in such a hurry. The thermometer has been stuck at over 90 degrees for a few days!

I told Elmer about the text, her recent visit to my house, and my conclusion that she wasn't so bad after all.

"You're pretty dense, dude" was all he said. I'm not sure what he means by that.

Good and Bad

We've been handing out fliers again this week. We're starting to recognize people that we've talked to before.

"We're lookin' out for those mitten crabs!" they holler to us as they tie up their boats.

Today, a man on the dock said, "Hey, kids, take a look at this thing." We went over to see what was in one of his crab pots. It wasn't a mitten; it was a mud crab. But it makes me feel good that people are on the lookout for mittens and that they trust us to inspect suspicious crabs they've caught.

The Mitten Watch website has had lots of activity but no definite IDs. In her lab's office by the marina, Dr. Mo let us listen to messages on the hotline, just for something different to do.

"I'm glad no one has found a mitten yet," Joey said. "I want us to be the first ones. Besides getting a First-to-Find badge, we'd probably be in the newspaper or interviewed on TV."

"You know, kids," Dr. Mo said, "as exciting it would be to find a mitten, it would be alarming too. It would mean they're invading our waters once again and messing up our ecosystem. As you know, once established they'd be extremely difficult to get rid of."

She had a point.

After a long, hot day on Tuesday, Margaux invited us all back to the hotel swimming pool. I didn't want to go.

"Ned doesn't know how to swim," Joey stage-whispered to Margaux. Everyone in the whole town probably heard her.

"He'd probably learn real fast," Elmer said. "You just haven't had time to take lessons, right, Ned?"

"I'll go," I said, ignoring both of them.

While we were tossing a beach ball around in the shallow end of the pool, Joey invited Margaux to go on the Waterman Legacy tourist boat tour that her parents work on.

Margaux asked if Joey should invite the guys.

"Let's just make it a girls' thing," Joey said.

I was glad she'd said that. I'd been on that tourist boat with Joey too many times to count.

Dante's Big News

I woke up early today to Dante banging on my bedroom door. My dad had let him in. He's been on my case about sleeping late ("The early bird catches the worm!"), so I think he was happy for an excuse to get me out of bed.

"My dad bought a boat," Dante said. "A big one. And he says he'll take the whole Science Squad crabbing!"

I wasn't fully awake, and I didn't quite believe him. But in true Dante fashion, he went on and on until I was finally convinced.

He told me his dad had been talking about buying a boat ever since they had moved to the Eastern Shore, but his mom had always said it wasn't in the budget. And some stuff about how his dad used to go crabbing as a kid. And how crabs you catch yourself are more delicious. His dad also bought three crab traps, a tool for measuring crabs (which is basically a ruler), and a whole mess of chicken necks for bait.

The best news is his dad can take the whole Squad out tomorrow!

His dad was taking *Aunt Baybe* out for her maiden voyage that morning. (Dante wouldn't say why that was the boat's name, except that it was a family joke.)

It's all set. Dante's dad, the Science Squad, and Dooley will hunt for mittens on the bay tomorrow! I can't wait!

Crabbing Chaos

We met Dante and his dad at the dock early this morning.

"It's going to be tight quarters with five of you mates and Dooley on board," Mr. Edwards said. "All of you need to wear life jackets, Dooley included, and you need to watch what you're doing."

We all chanted, "Aye, aye, Captain," in unison, and Dooley barked and wagged his tail. He was as excited as we were to be going out on the water.

"All hands on deck!" Mr. Edwards shouted, and we were off.

We all had jobs. I was in charge of baiting the traps with the chicken necks. Joey was in charge of lowering the traps into the water, pulling them back up, and dumping any captured crabs into the bushel baskets. Dante was in charge of returning the traps to me so I could rebait them and hand them to Joey. We had to move pretty fast. Elmer was in charge of looking in the baskets for mittens. And Margaux said she would hang on to Dooley.

It all started pretty good, but then we all began tripping over each other, and the lines that are used to lower the traps into the water got all tangled up. While we were trying to untangle them, a couple of crabs got out of a basket and began scraping around on the floor of the boat. Blue crabs are master escape artists. On top of everything else, the water was starting to get choppy.

"I shouldn't have had pancakes for breakfast," Dante moaned, and then he yacked them over the side. "I don't think I'll ever eat pancakes again," he said later.

"Neither will we," the rest of us said in unison.

At one point, I slipped and clonked Joey in the head with a trap. Joey dumped a trap with two giant crabs in it on Elmer, and one of them attached itself to his hair, which is pretty long. He said something in Spanish that he never did translate for us.

"Use your imaginations," he said.

Margaux freaked out when a crab crawled onto her sneaker. When she tried to pull it off, it pinched her. She let go of Dooley's collar so she could grab some ice, but instead of reaching into the cooler with drinks and human food, she put her hand into the one with the chicken necks. Dooley was very interested in those! "Eew, eew," she kept saying, all the while trying to wipe the chicken bits stuck on her fingers onto Dooley's coat.

"Margoo," Dante whispered to me.

"Not nice, pukehead," I whispered back. I was beginning to feel a little guilty that I ever called her that name behind her back.

Dooley started barking at some gulls that were following us and tried to jump overboard. With all of us

hanging on to him, we averted a major disaster. Can you imagine trying to pull a soaking-wet fifty-pound Chessie back into a moving boat?

"Tomorrow, I'm buying gloves at the tackle shop," Mr. Edwards growled. "And the dog stays home."

Dooley wasn't the only problem. Dante was measuring the blue crabs with that special tool his dad bought. It's illegal to keep small ones. You have to toss them back into the bay, which Dante was doing. Except, he missed a few times—I think on purpose. Little crabs were flying all over the boat.

"Whoops! Sorry!" he kept saying, laughing like crazy the whole time.

Dante's dad kept yelling at us to get hold of ourselves. One time, Elmer got up and wrapped his arms around Dante, and said "Don't worry, I've got a hold of ourselves, Mr. Edwards."

We motored back to the dock, then we helped wash down the boat and triple-checked the traps and baskets for mittens. Dante's dad was in a really good mood because, in spite of all the clowning around, we'd actually gotten almost a whole bushel of blue crabs.

"There is something extra delicious about crabs you catch yourself," he said. "Let's go cook these bad boys up."

It's always fun being out on the bay, but the only crabs we wanted to find were Chinese mitten crabs. And we didn't.

I'm starting to think this project may have not been the best idea after all.

BIG NEWS

Dr. Mo texted me today and asked if I could get the Squad together at 11:00 a.m. at the marina. She said she wanted to share some big news. We were going to meet on the docks at 10:00 anyway to hand out more "Free Help" ads.

When we all got there, she announced some really exciting news: SOMEONE FOUND A MITTEN CRAB! A guy crabbing along the Hudson River found one in his crab pot.

The information wasn't even on the Mitten Watch website yet, but she wanted to share the news with us. She had a photo of the crab in a glass jar. It looked like something from a science fiction movie, *Crustacean from Outer Space*.

"In New York and not here?" Joey huffed. She seemed to take it personally that New York beat us to the punch.

"That's right," Dr. Mo said, "and the New York authorities have verified that it's a mitten."

Joey asked the question, "So the hunt is over for us?"

"Not at all," Dr. Mo said. "We're definitely going to keep looking here." She reminded us how mittens first hitchhike, then migrate. She showed us a map on the office wall behind her. There were little crab icons to mark the spots where scientists suspect mittens are in the waters.

"As you can see, there are yellow question marks next to Maryland and California, but there's only one green exclamation point here, in New York." She pointed to the spot. "That signifies a confirmed finding."

"How did a mitten end up there?" Joey asked.

"Part of the Hudson River is an estuary like our bay, and it eventually flows into the Atlantic Ocean, just like our bay does. It's been invaded by mittens before. The last ones reported there were in 2014."

"Will you go up to New York to look for more mittens now?" I asked.

"No, I'll keep looking in our bay and its tributaries, just like I hope you all will," she said. "We'll let our colleagues in New York State cover the Hudson River."

We bombarded Dr. Mo with questions. Joey and Margaux wanted to know if it's a female and did it lay eggs. Dr. Mo said yes, a female, but female crabs don't usually lay their eggs until winter.

Dante wanted to know whether there were other crabs that got away. I guess he was remembering his and Elmer's frantic attempts to capture crabs on our first canoe trip. Dr. Mo said no other crabs were caught, but it wasn't likely the crab was hanging out all by herself. She also told us there was still a "distinct possibility" of finding mittens on the bay, but I didn't see how we had a chance to be the first ones—unless Dante's dad would take us out on *Aunt Baybe* again.

As we were walking home from the marina, I pointed out that our best chance of finding a mitten before anyone else around here did would be if we were on a boat.

"Yeah," Dante said. "I've GOT to convince my dad to take us out again, like soon."

That's just what I hoped he would say. I hope he can make it happen.

What a day! A mitten actually caught! Game on!

Man (Almost) Overboard!

Another trip on the bay!

In spite of his "obligations," Mr. Edwards agreed to take us out crabbing one more time this week—after that he needed to "buckle down" and get some writing done. This time, Mrs. Edwards kept Dooley with her, which made the day a whole lot more enjoyable.

Mr. Edwards bought us all heavy blue gloves to wear. We tried a new arrangement on the boat so the chicken-necks cooler was nearer to me. Since Dooley wasn't on board, Margaux suggested that her new job should be to sit next to me and help keep the trap lines from getting tangled.

The lines actually got more tangled last time when Joey was pulling the traps <u>up</u> out of the water and tossing them to Dante than when Joey was getting the traps from me and lowering them <u>down</u> into the water. I was about to point out the flawed logic when Elmer said, "That's a terrific idea, Margaux. Those tangled lines almost choked Ned last time."

I'm not even sure what he was talking about.

"Maybe we should try something besides chicken necks," Elmer said, suddenly the expert on tangled lines. "How do we know if mittens like them?"

Margaux agreed. "Maybe they would rather eat shrimp."

"Too expensive," Dante's dad said. "This trip isn't about the bait. It's about the fun of catching blue crabs for dinner. Unless we can *eat* mitten crabs. Can we?"

"Daaaad," Dante wailed. "I gave you and Mom the flier. No! It's not a good idea to eat them!"

We had our act together much more today, as far as an efficient assembly line went. But an embarrassing thing happened: I almost fell overboard.

Dante and I both left our posts at the same time. I went to see how many crabs and other stuff were in Elmer's basket, and Dante went to see if there were any snacks in the cooler. We tripped over each other; I lost my balance and started to fall over the side.

"Grab him! He can't swim!" Margaux yelled so loudly that I think EVERYONE on the bay heard.

Elmer leaped into action to pull me back onto the deck.

"No worries, he has a life jacket on," Joey said. "And he's fallen overboard lots of times before."

I'm sure that didn't help my image either.

I think Dante's dad was losing patience with us. But we did fill another basket with blue crabs, all of them alive and kicking.

"Their claws are sooo pretty," Margaux said. "I love that shade of blue."

"The females have red tips on their claws," Joey pointed out.

"Those are beautiful, too, like they're wearing nail polish."

"I agree," I said. "Did you know that the blue crab's scientific name, translated from Latin, means 'beautiful savory swimmer'?"

"It's the perfect name," Margaux said.

I agreed. A perfect name and a perfect day . . . except for almost falling overboard.

Shhhhh!

Secrets

I was at Dante's house this afternoon, waiting for him to clean up and change. We'd been riding our bikes, and Dante wanted to shower before we met Margaux at her pool. I didn't bother to go home to shower or grab swim trunks, because no way was I going in the water. Twice in a summer seems like overkill to me.

While I was killing time waiting for Dante, I looked at some brochures on the Edwards' coffee table. One had a schedule of concerts at the university's World Performing Arts Center (WPAC). There was stuff about dancers from Ireland, singers from Spain, musicians from Thailand, drummers from Ghana, you name it. Then I saw it—the one Mrs. Edwards had highlighted in orange.

"Chinese acrobats!" I shouted. I grabbed the brochure and raced into Mrs. Edwards's office. She and Mr. Edwards were wearing black sweat suits and spinning metal plates on long wooden poles in each hand.

When I barged in, they lost their concentration, I guess, and the plates went flying every which way and crashed to the floor.

"Um, excuse me for interrupting," I said, "but there are Chinese acrobats coming to the university?"

"Yes, there are, Ned," she said, putting aside the poles and stooping down to pick up a plate that had landed next to me. She seemed to move away from me quickly. Guess I smelled pretty ripe.

"Dante's dad and I are writing a book on acrobats," she said. "We're trying the spinning plates act for ourselves." (I couldn't imagine why, but I didn't want to ask). "Of course, we're not agile enough to try the rest of their fabulous feats. Are you interested in acrobats?"

"No," I said. "I mean, yes! I mean, I'm interested in Chinese acrobats."

"Oh right," she said, "because of your special interest in Chinese mitten crabs and Chinese warriors. Well, these acrobats are of special interest to Dante's dad"—she pointed to him—"because as a kinesiologist, he studies how energy moves in our bodies and things that might block it. We all want our bodies to use energy as efficiently as possible, right? That energy is what the Chinese call 'chi'."

I'd seen acrobats performing on high wires at the circus. Probably no one has more pumped-up chi than they do! And these were acrobats coming to our town!

Mr. Edwards kind of slinked out of the room, but Mrs. Edwards was still talking: "The acrobats are the opening act on this season's roster at the WPAC. It's a one-night performance on Saturday night. They're staying at the Edgewater Resort. Didn't Margaux mention it? You kids should come with us and meet them ahead of time. And, of course, come to the show."

"Definitely! Thanks!" An idea was starting to bubble up in my chi-charged brain.

Just then, Dante flew into the office, decked out in flowered trunks and a matching shirt. "You smell gross, my man," Dante said.

I chose to be the bigger person and did not comment on how ridiculous he looked.

"Let's just get going," I said.

When we got to the hotel, I told the Squad I'd have to sit this one out—I didn't have my swimsuit. Margaux

waved her hand in front of her face as if she was
clearing the air and said it was "probably a good idea."

Dante snickered. I just shrugged.

I set up operations for the afternoon at a picnic
table in a nice shady area surrounded with what were
probably invasive plants, and thought about Operation
Acrobats. There were three things I wanted to find out:

1. Is the performance free?

2. Can we invite as many people as we like?

3. Can we pass out fliers on mittens at the
*   performance and talk about what we've learned?*

I figured even if we never find any mittens, we
could at least talk about them and maybe still get our
Invasive Species badges.

Margaux tapped me on the shoulder and jolted me
out of my thoughts.

"Hey, can I talk to you for a minute?" she asked.

"Um, sure," I said.

"I'm moving to Montana at the end of summer," she
blurted out.

I just stared at her, unsure of what to say.

She must have sensed my discomfort, because she added, "I figured I should tell you as the leader of the Squad."

"Why?" I finally managed to ask.

She told me how her parents were divorced and how moving every few months with her mom's job has been hard on her. So it was decided that she'd move to Montana to live with her dad.

I asked her how long she'd known, and she said knew it when she came to Edgewater. She'll spend the summers with her mom, wherever she is. She didn't want to say anything to us, because we might not have let her into the Science Squad if we found she was leaving at the end of the summer.

I told her that was ridiculous.

She looked miserable. "Everywhere we move, I feel like an outsider. I try really hard to fit in. Sometimes, too hard, I guess."

Looking back at the events of this summer, I can see that now.

Dante was headed our way, carrying chips and sodas.

"Please don't tell anyone," she whispered.

"Do you have allergies?" he asked when he plopped himself down at our table.

Her eyes were red, and she was blowing her nose. "It's the chorine in the pool," she said.

I don't know what to do. I don't want to blab her secret if she doesn't want me to, but I think the Squad should know. But in the end, I want to be Margaux's friend. So I'll keep my mouth shut.

EUREKA!

This morning, Mr. Edwards took us all out on the bay again.

"How about if we try a river instead of the bay, Dad?" Dante suggested. "That's where they caught a mitten in New York."

"I'm more interested in where folks are catching blue crabs right now."

"I just checked the fishing report yesterday, Captain Edwards," Elmer said. "The blues are hot right now on the Accohannock River."

So that's where we went. Talk about acrobats! We were totally coordinated moving around the boat. Mr. Edwards didn't yell at us once.

Margaux hadn't had a chance to look through the basket for mittens yet, so she asked Elmer if she could try it today. Elmer just shrugged and said okay.

We were pretty far up the river when Margaux said, "Hey, I think I found one!"

"Probably a spider crab," Elmer muttered.

"No, for real!" she said frantically and reached in to grab her find. She held it up by its back legs, which I didn't think she would ever have the nerve to do. It definitely wasn't a blue crab. It definitely wasn't a spider crab. It had furry claws and a little notch between its eyes. EUREKA! Margaux found a Chinese mitten crab!

"Dad!" Dante shouted. "Where are we?"

"The planet Earth so far as I can tell, son."

"No! I mean can you check your GPS and give us your exact location? We think we've caught a mitten!"

"Make that three!" Joey shouted as she pulled up another trap and dumped the contents into a basket. "Two mittens and one blue crab."

Holy crab!

I took a ton of pictures and sent them to Dr. Mo.

She texted back right away. "I think you've hit the jackpot. Put them on ice and get back to the marina as soon as you can. I'll meet you there."

To celebrate our find, Mr. Edwards wanted to pull into a sandy cove and eat our lunches. But we said there was no way were we willing to do that. We were reaching the pinnacle of our scientific mission.

"We have to get back to the marina as fast as possible," I said.

"Looks like I've got a mutiny on my hands," Mr. Edwards said good-naturedly.

All the way back, we were supposed to keep catching more blue crabs. We tried our best, but it was hard to concentrate. We were so distracted. Three times, Joey let traps filled with gigantic blue crabs overturn, sending them splashing back into the river. That was partly my fault, because instead of helping with the traps, I carried the three mittens over to the chicken-necks cooler, tossed them in, and covered them with ice. "Enjoy your last meal, guys," I said.

After that, we all pretty much abandoned our official duties and kept looking at the mittens. We couldn't believe our eyes. WE DID IT!

"Not even a third of a bushel this time," Mr. Edwards chuckled when we eased into his boat slip. "What happened?"

"Mitten crabs happened, Dad!" Dante said.

Dr. Mo and her whole staff were on the dock waiting for us. Everyone was cheering and clapping.

"Permission to come aboard, Captain," she said to Mr. Edwards. "I need to secure your mitten cargo."

She climbed aboard and put each mitten into a plastic bag. "We'll freeze these right away and rush them to the main lab for analysis," she said. "But there's no mistaking those furry claws, is there?"

There sure isn't. After all of our campaigning and searching through wetlands and streams, finding a mitten was awesome!

Operation Acrobats

I think I would be going crazy waiting for the results of the lab analysis if I didn't have Operation Acrobats to distract me.

Mrs. Edwards texted a big, fat "YES" to my three questions from before. She loved the idea of us talking to the audience about the mittens.

At our Squad meeting, we talked about what we wanted to say and how to get the word out about the performance. The university has been advertising the event on social media and putting up colorful posters about it all over campus and around town. But now the show wasn't going to be just acrobats, it was going to be informing the public about mittens.

Mittens Verified

Our primo captures were mittens all right! We got the news from Dr. Mo this morning. We sent in our applications right away to get our official Invasive Species badges. We wanted to make sure we'd be able to show them off at the Chinese acrobats' show.

Summer is ending soon, but the hunt for mittens won't. Because of their catadromous life cycle, they'll always be moving around somewhere. Dr. Mo had told us that mitten larvae, like blue crab larvae, are microscopic. And that juvenile mittens can be the size of a pea while they're feeding on other plankton and getting ready for their migrations to fresh water. So, some seasons are better than others for finding them.

Maybe Joey and I can talk our middle school science teacher into mitten-finding field trips in the fall, when hordes of adults could be heading back downstream to the bay.

Opening Act

When I was at Dante's house today, Mrs. Edwards said to figure on being on stage for about five minutes before the acrobats took over. I'm not sure why I hadn't thought that far ahead—that talking to the audience would involve me getting on stage. Eek!

She also said it's a large auditorium, so we could invite as many people as we liked. That gave me a lot to think about. We had to decide who we wanted to invite, make sure people knew our mittens talk was going to be part of the show, and decide what to say in our five minutes on stage.

I made a list of everyone we wanted to tell (or warn?!).

"This is going to be impossible," Dante said.

"No, it won't be," I said. "Crowdsourcing, remember? We can drum up lots of enthusiasm for the acrobats and for our presentation. We text our friends, we tell *our parents, and ask them to tell their friends. And you know Dr. Mo is going to be excited about it."*

Dante said his mom and dad had already been telling everyone about the performance because of their book, but that they'll want to add that their son is giving a presentation on Chinese mitten crabs before the performance.

Right . . .

I was pretty sure my dad would mention it to his friends and their families and to his decoy-carving buddies. And I could count on my mom to invite the whole hospital staff. Elmer said he'd ask his dad to spread the news at the seafood processing plant and to extend a special invitation to that nice older lady we talked with, the one who's been dismembering crabs for forty years. Margaux said there were already posters at the hotel front desk, in the restaurants, and near the pool, and she guaranteed her mom will personally spread the word to the whole staff and all the guests.

Joey added that she needed to email Mr. Reinholt anyway with a few more questions about his cargo ships, so she'd be sure to invite him and his workers to the show.

"So, who's left?" I asked. "Tourists, shopkeepers, restaurant owners. We're walking around town, talking with them all the time anyway. This is exciting news to tell them about." I added that in case they hadn't seen them already, we could hand out those flashy posters about the acrobats' show.

Wow! We could pull in a big crowd. I hope Dante's mom meant it when she said we could invite whoever we wanted.

I think we've done a stellar job of telling people what the mittens look like and what to do if they find one. But just to be sure, I said we should hand out Dr. Mo's fliers one last time, as people piled into the auditorium. And I still had that box of bumper stickers she gave us awhile back. We could give those out too!

I still can't believe we're going to be the opening act for the acrobats. What a super way to raise awareness about mittens!

Our Plan

Today, we decided what we would talk about before the acrobatics show. Elmer will start by talking about how we toured Dr. Mo's research vessel, searched under docks, slogged through the wetlands, and paddled up streams. Then Dante will talk about how we went crabbing on the bay.

I'll jump in and say how it was hard, slow work. But that we persisted because we were Guardians of the Bay, and if the Chinese mitten crabs were invading our waters, we needed to track them down.

And then we'll turn to the big screen behind us to show the presentation that Joey and Margaux put together of the pictures of us with the mittens.

And, of course, we decided we'd wear the Invasive Species badges we earned.

It's all settled. And it's going to be great!

Knitting Mittens?!
Seriously?

This morning, Margaux had another idea for the performance. She thinks we need something that everyone can take home with them after the show to "remind them to remain vigilant" (her words).

"That sounds like a good idea, like rubber wristbands," I said. I wanted to make sure I was being supportive. I mean, who doesn't like a good wristband for awareness?!

Margaux had another idea. "Those could be attractive, but we'd have to buy those. What I was thinking was something that we make ourselves. Then we could get Creativity stickers." She whipped out a pair of mittens she was hiding behind her back. "I vote that we knit mittens in three sizes: small, medium, and large. We'll say something like: 'Wear your mittens to remember the mittens!'"

Dante snickered, and I just stared at her, open-mouthed. Was she serious? I know I promised to be nicer, but really?!

Joey was all for the mittens idea, and Elmer said knitting wasn't just for girls, so he was fine with it.

I couldn't believe it. I thought it was a terrible idea (still do!). But with a vote of three to two, it was decided.

The Guardians of the Bay are knitting mittens.

Help.

Knitting Mittens. Seriously.

Margaux's mom took Margaux and Joey shopping, and bought knitting needles and bunches (called "skeins") of stretchy "crab-blue" yarn. They set up camp in a conference room at the hotel. It was air-conditioned, and there were great snacks, but that may have been the only reasons that Dante and I were there . . .

We took the needles Margaux assigned to us and hid out in a corner of the lobby. It was a perfect spot: out of the way, so not many people noticed us, but still inside and out of the terrible heat. And it turns out, knitting needles make great swords and burrow jabbers.

While we were messing around with our knitting swords, Joey appeared out of nowhere. Guess it wasn't that hidden after all. She was hopping mad.

"You guys are such jerks," she said.

"Knitting not going well?" I asked.

"No, it's not, smart aleck. Knitting mittens takes time. We've only finished ten pairs so far, and the performance is Saturday."

"What's taking you so long?" Dante asked.

I saw Joey take a deep breath and (probably) silently count to ten. "For one thing, there's only three of us working our fingers to the bone on what's supposed to be a team effort. And some of the mittens are turning out . . . misshapen. Elmer's making a total mess of the ones he's done, and Margaux's having a meltdown. She's locked herself in a linen closet at the hotel."

Okay, so I felt pretty bad about that. I still wasn't sure knitting mittens was the best idea, but we are a team. And if the team decided this was a good idea, I (especially as the leader) should join them.

"We'd better hustle back there and apologize," I said to Dante.

Knitting mittens wasn't easy. But Margaux was very patient as she taught us how. And she didn't even act superior when I made mistakes—and I made some whoppers on my first tries.

Everyone seemed to relax a little after the mittens started to pile up. Margaux suggested we give them to the acrobats and their coach first, and then to the first twenty or so people to arrive, depending on how many we could knit. She even went so far as to say we could take orders from anyone else who wanted a pair and maybe to ask for contributions that we could donate to charity.

Those are good ideas, but I'm not feeling confident we can knit that many by Saturday. My fingers are still hurting from all that effort today. It's even hard to hold a pen and write all this down. But we get to tag along with Dante's parents tonight and meet the acrobats. I can't wait!

Meeting the Acrobats!

The acrobats were the coolest! After a long day of knitting, it was nice to be doing something that didn't involve my hands.

I talked to one of them, Li, for a long time. Turns out that Li has been to see the Terra-Cotta Army! He told me that the famous Terra-Cotta Army wasn't all warriors. Some were musicians and acrobats. I'm not sure how I didn't come across that in my research. How fascinating!

But the best news is that after we explained our project, they said they would improvise a special scene for us. I don't know what that means, but I can't wait to find out!

The Big Performance

So much to say about today. Us on stage wearing our badges. An award! An epic battle! Handmade mittens. A promise to spread the news. A secret revealed. But let me start at the beginning.

Practically the whole town turned out for the performance. In the end we only made enough pairs of mittens to give the acrobats, but Margaux set up a table with a pair of sample mittens (with the best-looking pair!) and an order form. That was a good idea.

I was super nervous when we got up to talk. I could never be an actor. I almost tripped when it was my turn to take the microphone from Dante!

But everyone clapped for us, and our parents all stood up and cheered. We were about to go back to our seats when Dr. Mo came on stage and gave us each a citizen scientist award from her research lab. None of us were expecting it! More rounds of applause!

The acrobats were AMAZING. But the most amazing part was how they somehow made themselves look like crabs in this battle scene. At least, I thought they looked like crabs, but I guess I have been thinking a lot about crabs lately! The acrobats wrapped in brown scarves (which make me think of mittens) tried to invade the territory of other acrobats wrapped in blue scarves (which made me think of blue crabs)—AND LOST. Epic battle!

Afterward, Margaux presented the acrobats with the mittens that we had knitted for them. We all posed for pictures on stage.

And the best part is the acrobats promised to take fliers with them and pass them out to audiences on the rest of their US tour. Talk about a great way to spread the word!

After the crowd left and the acrobats were packing up their stuff, a few people hung around, talking about how terrific it all was.

I was feeling pretty great until I spotted Margaux sitting by herself, eyes puffy and red and a balled-up tissue in her hand.

I grabbed Elmer and motioned to Joey and Dante. "Hey, guys," I said, "look at Margaux. We need to go talk with her." I wondered if she would finally spill her secret.

"What's the matter, Marg?" Joey asked, putting her arm around her.

Margaux was crying so hard it took her awhile to say what was wrong.

"I'm moving to Montana in two weeks," she said shakily. "My mom's going to open a new hotel. She's not sure exactly what state yet. So I'm going to live with my dad. I'm not going to school here, and I'll have to quit the Science Squad."

Everyone looked shocked. Joey must not have known either!

"Montana isn't that far," Dante finally said.

Sob.

"Maybe you could come back here in the summer," Elmer said.

Sob.

"There are Science Squads all over the United States. I bet you'll be able to find one to join in Montana," Joey said.

Sob.

"I know for a fact that Montana has tons of great arrowheads," I said.

Margaux must like arrowheads even more than I thought. That was the only thing that seemed to cheer her up.

"Really, Ned?"

"Absolutely."

"Maybe you could come out and visit me, and we could look for them together, since we won't have a chance now to look for any here."

"Maybe . . . " I said. I'm not sure how THAT would work.

Elmer kicked me in the shin. It hurt! "She likes you, man," he whispered. "You should definitely go!"

Huh?

"You'll always be an honorary member of the Guardians of the Bay," I said. "That won't change."

That made Margaux start crying again.

Geez. I was trying to be nice. I don't understand girls at all.

Margaux wasn't the only one who was distressed. Joey got all worked up about the mitten orders. We'd gotten fifty orders and planned to donate any profits to the Preserve the Bay Foundation. "How are we going to do this without you, Margaux?" she moaned.

"We're going to have to have long-distance Science Squad knit-a-thons, that's all," Margaux said. "I'll keep knitting mittens in Montana and find some way to get them back to you."

Elmer told Margaux that he and his dad were leaving soon too. He also said he's taking a pack of fliers back with him to Mexico.

"Mittens have been in the San Francisco Bay before. If they migrate to Mexico, I'll be ready for them," he said. He made a fierce martial arts pose and gave her a wide smile. That made Margaux laugh.

Dante announced he wants our project next year to be about stormwater runoff, and he'll keep Margaux posted.

Joey said in middle school she wants to focus on ballast water issues. It's her thing now, ballast water.

I'm sticking with my plan to be an archaeologist, but I haven't decided about anything else. Maybe I'll focus next on how I can travel to China. I still believe that fortune cookie message is true. I am going to step on the soil there someday.

But in the meantime, I'll figure out a way to get to Montana to visit Margaux. I think my dad would agree that it's probably a great spot to search for arrowheads. And Margaux really isn't bad. We've had a lot of fun together. Plus, because of her, we found the mitten crabs!

Animal Name: Chinese mitten crab (*Eriocheir sinensis*)

What's happening? Chinese mitten crab larvae are unintentionally carried in the ballast water of oceangoing vessels and transferred to non-native waters. It's also possible that Chinese mitten crabs have been traded illegally.

Why are they so destructive? Chinese mitten crabs, when not in their native habitat, compete for food and habitat with other aquatic species such as the blue crab. They can destroy the nets and steal the bait of fishers. They can cause serious erosion and clog water systems.

Why is stopping them so challenging? These crabs can travel up to 800 miles and can walk on land if they encounter traps, dams, or other obstacles in the water. Like other invasive species, once established, they can spread quickly and be nearly impossible to get rid of. They can also be elusive, thus very hard to spot in the wild.

How can you help? Educate yourself and others on how to identify a Chinese mitten crab and how to proceed if you do find one. DO NOT throw these critters back into the water. And always thoroughly clean boat hulls and fishing gear before moving to another area. This is an effective way to protect waters from all aquatic hitchhikers.

In the Field

Darrick Sparks, a biological technician with Smithsonian Environmental Research Center (SERC) in Edgewater, Maryland, is on a mission to track the Chinese mitten crab.

Sparks monitors the spread and establishment of invasive species. He and his colleagues set up a hotline and online tracking system called Mitten Crab Watch. They received dozens of reports from 2005 through 2009. After that, nothing.

"Invasive species usually don't disappear, but we thought maybe we just got lucky. More likely, though, the Chinese mittens crabs never left. People just stopped looking for them. This time, we launched an all-out effort to find them, urging citizens to join us. We figured with all of that water, someone should see something."

And someone did while on the Hudson River near Yonkers in May 2018. A crabber reported finding a live adult male Chinese mitten crab in his crab pot to the New York authorities, who then contacted SERC. It was the first capture reported to SERC since the relaunch of its "Find the Mittens" campaign in 2018.

"Now that we know they're here," Sparks says, "we need to determine if they're breeding and, if so, how we can keep their numbers down. We'll be working on a battle plan."

Glossary

brackish – *A combination of fresh and salt water. Most of the water in the Chesapeake Bay is brackish.*

carapace – *A hard shell, also called an exoskeleton, that covers the back of an animal, such as a crab. It provides support and protection in invertebrates.*

catadromous – *Migrating between salty and fresh water.*

estuary – *A partially enclosed body of water where fresh water from rivers and streams mixes with salt water from the ocean. It is an area of transition from land to sea.*

fouling community – *The diverse assortment of organisms that cling to boats and underwater structures such as piers.*

invasive species – *Plants and animals that are introduced, whether accidentally or on purpose, into a new environment, where they have a negative impact on native species and/or human activities.*

invertebrate – *An animal that does not have a backbone. Crabs are one example.*

molt – *When an animal sheds its hard shell. Chinese mitten crabs, blue crabs, and other crustaceans have to molt in order to grow.*

setae – *Patches of bristles (pronounced see-tee) like those that give the Chinese mitten crab its distinct appearance.*

spawn – *To release eggs and/or sperm into the water.*

Selected Bibliography

Collard, Sneed B. *Science Warriors: The Battle Against Invasive Species*. Boston: Houghton Mifflin, 2008.

"*Learn the Issues. Invasive Species*." Chesapeake Bay Program, chesapeakebay.net/issues/invasive_species. Accessed June 2018.

"*Top Ten Suspects. Chinese Mitten Crab. Morty the Menace*." Sea Grant Illinois-Indiana, iiseagrant.org/NabInvader/Pacific/suspects/moreinfo_morty.html. Accessed June 2018.

"*Welcome to Mitten Crab Watch*." Smithsonian Environmental Research Center, mittencrab.nisbase.org. Accessed June 2018.

About the Author

Mary C. Wild and her family live in Maryland, not far from the Chesapeake Bay, a national treasure that she enjoys sharing stories about with readers. She writes fiction for children and for the young at heart.

About the Consultant

Dr. Andrew David is a marine biologist at Clarkson University. His main area of research involves the development of genetic and biophysical methods for tracking the spread of aquatic invasive species. At Clarkson, he teaches a variety of animal biology courses, including Introductory Zoology, Parasitology, and Marine Biology. He currently resides in Parishville, New York.

About the Illustrator

Arpad Olbey is an illustrator veteran and art director of his art studio in London. He works with paper, pencils, and paints, or digital high-tech equipment, depending on the project. His wish is to combine his experience and technical knowledge to deliver the best that his creativity can give to audiences.

Nocturnal Symphony:

A Bat Detector's Journ.

by J. A. Watson

Illustrated by
Arpad Olbey

Hardcover ISBN:
978-1-63163-299-0

Paperback ISBN:
978-1-63163-300-3

Brubeck Farrell has two problems: her Science Squad needs money to buy bat detection equipment, and she needs to convince her mom to marry her longtime girlfriend. Will Bru's fundraising and matchmaking efforts eventually pay off?

AVAILABLE NOW